CU00590266

Quantum Narratives

Dimensional Verse in Passion's Wavelength

Benjamin Vaccaro

Quantum Narratives

Dimensional Verse in Passion's Wavelength

(First Edition)

Benjamin Vaccaro

Publisher: Benjamin Vaccaro - 1-D Boxwood Road - Port Washington, NY 11050

Quantum Narratives

Copyright © 2020 by Benjamin Vaccaro.

All rights reserved. The following manuscript is a compilation of poems. Some works are fictionalized (from real-life events) others are wholly fictional (from the author's creativity). With the exception of brief quotations in a book review, no part of this book may be replicated, stored in a retrieval system, or transmitted in any form, or by any means, electronic, mechanical, photocopying, recording, or otherwise, without prior written permission of the author.

First Printing, 2020
Vaccaro, Benjamin Thomas, 1956 –
Library of Congress Control Number (LCCN): 2020917023

Publisher's Cataloging-in-Publication Data

Names: Vaccaro, Benjamin, author.
Title: Quantum narratives : dimensional verse in passion's wavelength / Benjamin Vaccaro.
Description: Port Washington, NY: Benjamin Vaccaro, 2020.
Identifiers: ISBN: 978-1-7353909-0-1 (pbk.) | 978-1-7353909-1-8 (pdf) | 978-1-7353909-2-5 (epub) | 978-1-7353909-3-2 (mobi)
Subjects: LCSH Experimental fiction. | Poetry, American. | Short Stories, American. | BISAC FICTION / Literary
Classification: LCC PS3622 .A31 Qu3 2020 | DDC 811-ddc23

Author - Benjamin Vaccaro: (https://www.benjaminvaccaro.com)
Publisher - Benjamin Vaccaro: 1-D Boxwood Rd - Pt Washington, NY 11050

10 9 8 7 6 5 4 3 2 1

To my Mother and Father, wishing they were here

And my Brother, fortunate he is

Author's Blah, Blah, Blah...

There is a proverb I use often: *It is not the guest that should thank the host for inviting, but the host, the guest, for coming.*

So, sisters, brothers, and humans of any stripe, welcome to my first book, and kind thanks. Your company is an honor.

Ya' know how we watch the same movie (or a scene from one) multiple times, or play a certain song, attend the same musical act, play, opera, museum, ballet, and so on? I do; I do it all the time. With this custom in mind, I sought to create a book, of varying length stories, to which a reader periodically returns, owing to its memorable features (assuming it has any).

Rather than plain-spoken stories, I chose rhyming poetry as the format, mainly because of the following:

1. Its license to wander into the territory of metaphor
2. It's more "forgiving" with: polysyllabic words, altering parts of speech, grammatical latitude, word order, punctuation, and "creative" spelling
3. It's more like a "song"
4. It permits a higher degree of complexity
5. It requires research, and I absorb in the process

Continuing my "music" reference: there are short ditties, and there are magnum opuses (symphonies) demanding an extended span of attention. I "compose" both (and all in-between) from the 1-minute to the 1-hour read. Poetized with a touch of eloquence, perhaps herein is a composition worthy of a second look.

Benjamin Vaccaro

Rhyming poetry, in today's market, comes with the inherent risk of sounding like a nursery rhyme; however traditional adult verse, endeavors to transcend juvenile embellishments, by judicious use of metaphor, earmarked vocabularies, poetic density, imagery, meter, and so on, where the total becomes greater than the sum of its parts. It's a high-wire act I have yet to conquer, but, done astutely, momentous poetry rises.

It's all theater: I want you to enjoy the drama, and "hear" the lines as I do when I'm drafting them; but I'm wedged between explaining how I write, without it appearing like a lesson on how to read. Anyway, with a well-mannered approach, I'll chance it and mention a few nuances, in the architecture, that may help the lines mature, from so-so to appetizing; small adjustments divide these extremes. I may never get such an opportunity again, so, with your permission:

In mathematics the tilde (~) means *approximately*. In this manuscript, I don't use it that way. Here, it has a threefold purpose (PPP - pace, pause, & pitch):

1) Pace - pace up to the tilde
2) Pause - pause with a bit of drama (*ya' know I'm Italian, and we turn everything into an opera*)
3) Pitch - drop your pitch. The tonality diminishes on the right side of the tilde.

Besides, I'm big on aesthetics of text. I think the tilde offers an easy "look" to the poetic line. A meal just tastes better, when it looks better; presentation is central.

Another subtlety you may notice, for example, lines A, B, and C, where line B completes A's thought, but it also opens C's thought. This duality is an orderly, unintended consequence of overthinking. When I noticed it, I left it alone, betting the oddity draws more praise than scorn. Let's hope...

Lastly, it's pentameter-ish (except for *The Eyes inside My Lids*). And yes, I have a few breaks in continuity where forced rhyming, and stubborn accenting, are needed.

Words: Some say, keep them simple and speak candidly. Others say, all words are there for our use, so use them. So who's right? Probably everyone. Here's my take:

This is poetry (or, at least, that's its intent) with pointed distinctions from a novel, newspaper column, and most common written media. I approach certain elements of poetry as though I was writing a proverb, in that it should tell more with less (maximum import with minimal words – parsimony). Natural law only permits us to blow a spherical bubble (maximum volume with minimum material, or surface area). Think Ockham's razor. Nature doesn't waste. I say: when composing, emulate nature, and parsimoniously draw upon various lexica. Overdoing the metaphor, and it'll sound like that topic; underdoing it, restricts poetic license. *Find the balance and go for it!*

Thanks for listening - Enjoy!

Table of Contents

A Romantic Poet

I mused I was ~ a romantic poet
Where seed-like letters ~ bud flowery words
And gardened stanzas ~ in detail show it
As tuneful phrases ~ are mimicked by birds
And love's majesty ~ easily bestirred

  Irrigating thirst ~ of quixotic needs
  Sweet words as water ~ verses, new sprung seeds

Treetop feathers sing ~ and honeybees buzz
Words vivify staves ~ and dormant gardens
Metaphors de-ice ~ all lawless cold does
And arbitrates *frost* ~ all lawful pardons
Unstiffening which ~ wintertime hardens

  Fluidic expressions ~ similes sprout
  Aqueous imagery ~ offsetting drought

My wording would be ~ thoughtfully lettered
And all inflection ~ pleasingly aural
So much, grammarians ~ neither bettered
Nor choirmaster ~ resound more choral
Or magnetic sky ~ glow more auroral

  Perhaps (by my work) ~ warring sects be-doved
  Then for peaceful pen ~ ever I be loved

Finis

Breakfast Symphony

Morning's frequencies ~ captivate my heart
By melodic wings ~ that (daybreak) blesses
Nonviolent feathers ~ chirping peaceful art
Cooing harmony ~ 'twixt short recesses
And when my eyes ope, ~ I identify
Consonant phrasing ~ to inspire love
Canopied lyricists ~ syllabify
A duet for ~ the Nightingale and dove
One overtures with ~ a stand-alone ping
A second echoes ~ in three-quarter verse
But after eight measures ~ more flock to sing
Breakfast symphonies ~ wholly unrehearsed

Being aural witness ~ to daybreak's song
Urging the authors: ~ *each stanza, prolong*

Finis

Decimation of the English

I'm a foreigner ~ in my native village
Assailed by legions ~ of contrastive tongues
Accents and spelling ~ are nearly pillaged
As diction's ladder ~ holds uncivil rungs
Out grammar's window ~ kingly English bungs

  Hollow expressions ~ of verbosity
  Lacking cerebral ~ curiosity

Some charge I export ~ high magniloquence
Fostering commerce ~ in well-spoken trade
Others traffic syntax ~ of stultiloquence
Like words seized in ~ a tongue-tied barricade
Desisting import ~ by oral blockade

  Deporting ideas ~ best left unspoken
  Wishing their silence ~ remained unbroken

And when addressing ~ our stylish youth
I offer my face ~ to distracted teens
(Who divide their thoughts ~ mum chided uncouth)
My eyes viewing scalps ~ theirs transfixed on screens
With a random peek ~ in the in-betweens

  Mind-numbing drivel ~ by tongues, unfettered
  Originating ~ in minds, unlettered

Irrational tongues ~ belch lip-flapping noise
Doping my ears ~ on witless platitudes
Worthless phrasing ~ (in sub-standard poise)
Accompanied by ~ equal attitudes
And unconnected ~ dumb vicissitudes

Unintelligible ~ ideation
Breeds hyperbolic ~ exaggeration

Sensationalizing ~ compositions
Journalists vending ~ headlines bombastic
Ending sentences ~ in prepositions
Media stories ~ beyond fantastic
As tho' rigid facts ~ were of elastic

And Churchill's poetic ~ metrical foot
Was something up with ~ which he would not put

Some nearby gadgets ~ barge in on dinner
Kids gracelessly text ~ while I'm out eating
Tho' I wear smiles, ~ patience wears thinner
As 'twixt each nibble ~ I hear them tweeting
Pyrrhus's Romans ~ were not worth beating

They thumbed a dummies guide ~ on how to sext:
Addictive Habits ~ by Yule B. Nekst

If fluency sports ~ the garb of grammar
Then commentators ~ should dress-up like clowns
Adulterous verbs ~ lure with see-thru glamour
Phony articles ~ diaphanous gowns
Unwed conjugates ~ disloyal to nouns

  I listen daily ~ with endless loathing
  Knowing treason bleeds ~ sheer thru their clothing

Promiscuous mouths ~ shamelessly saying
A masculine form ~ whoring with Miss-Spelled
A feral voice box ~ in need of spaying
While proper linguistic ~ justly rebelled
Asking rhetoricians ~ that the gelder geld

  Unruly verses ~ of lines untutored
  Confirms errant tongues ~ are best off neutered

Then I queried ~ an old dictionary
And Middle English- ~ type Librarian
Both referenced *The Tales ~ from Canterbury*
Penned by one ~ time-honored grammarian
Not Shakespearean ~ most Chaucerian

  Whose shrewd assignment ~ instructed to vowels
  Charmed verses in ~ *The Parlement of Foules*

Talk radio pukes ~ verbal diarrhea
When ominous facts ~ stay unpublicized
Newspapers issue ~ daily logorrhea
And with their surplus ~ (gardens) fertilize
Miss Marilyn's death ~ they eroticized

  Sidetracking writers ~ (of excrement) full
  Annotations authored ~ by Fuller Bull

We've debased spelling ~ to simple phonics
Go on promoting ~ unearned diplomas
Larynxes hacking ~ diseased mnemonics
Spewing oratory ~ carcinomas
With choked-out meaning ~ taught by Miss Nomers

  Modern instructors, ~ when they should demote
  Not surprisingly, ~ without care, promote

One lettered biped ~ (majesty) composed
Deeply endowed ~ with writing genetics
Drafted by fingers ~ rightly juxtaposed
The honeyed rhyme of ~ William's poetics
Where unsweetened ears ~ become diabetics

  Critically down, ~ our language is dumbed
  'Tis hard to think ~ we're opposable-thumbed

From the Pliocene ~ arose glossaries
And Hominids grew ~ (thru time) loquacious
Now some voice fiction, ~ some state verities
So when asked her age ~ Lucy spoke veracious
Eons (of a birth) ~ after Cretaceous

  'Cause neighboring bones ~ to her maxillary
  Expanded human ~ vocabulary

Ignorance employs ~ low-priced expletives
Witlessness hires ~ the dated cliché
But over-indulgence ~ on adjectives
Means poets have nothing ~ profound to say
And should consider ~ rehab from A-A

  A twelve-step program ~ that's synonymous
  With *cured* at Adjectives ~ Anonymous

To vile grammar ~ librettos succumbed
The savvy stanza ~ (and sweet verse) corrodes
Some trendy lyrics ~ sound better hummed
Since they intonate ~ in asinine codes
To our lost language ~ I chant wistful odes

  Melodies challenged ~ with un-clarity
  As harmonies reek ~ of vulgarity

If Mother English ~ is to bring forth young
Let Byron be ~ the inseminator
Such that the offspring ~ (by eloquent tongue)
Boast wholesome traits ~ of their procreator
Or Barnfield perhaps ~ a term donator

  Today some speak ~ in such overblown words
  That, their seconds my firsts, ~ their sixths my thirds

Finis

Indecent Exposure

With benefit from ~ shrewd statisticians
Some uncovered ~ by extrapolation
Telecom players ~ buy politicians
With evil aims ~ for Earth's population
By puking harmful ~ Wi-Fi emissions
Bathing humankind ~ in radiation

In 1984 ~ Blair[1] theorized
With human spirit ~ fully weaponized
5G technologies ~ actualize

Tower to tower ~ spreading vile rumors
In obscene bandwidths ~ of profanity
Marching to pulses ~ (soldiered consumers)
Taking commands ~ from Chief Insanity
In false flag wavelengths ~ creating tumors
Or friendly fire ~ on humanity

Insolent gossip ~ (lacking decency)
In pejorative ~ wordless frequency
Morphing fit cells into ~ malignancy

From children's toys ~ to printers wireless
The blue tooth tablet ~ and untethered phones
Baby monitors ~ ignitions keyless
SMART devices ~ taint surrounding zones
Constant bombardment ~ from routers tireless
Giving innocents ~ oncogenic bones

Microwave ovens, ~ iPads, and 'droids
Fragmentary truth ~ written in the 'bloids
Altering humans ~ into humanoids

Low intensity ~ and non-ionic
Phones in breast pockets, ~ pads comfy in laps
Inches distant ~ from the embryonic
Penetrating skin ~ as the unborn naps
Misuse of knowledge ~ truly demonic
Naïve patrons stray ~ into corporate traps

But fractional truth ~ is a total lie
Without minutiae ~ one cannot ask: *why*
Into our bodies ~ their frequencies pry

Vibrations maintain ~ an unbroken sweep
From the basinet ~ to the working space
It's there when awake ~ and thru soundest asleep
And every extreme ~ in your living place
Roaming aimlessly ~ un-shepherded sheep
As the gullible ~ discover no trace

  (Led to the slaughterhouse ~ like guiltless cattle)
  A species ensnared ~ in soundless battle
  'Twixt towers screaming ~ cancerous prattle

DNA-altering ~ frequency bands
Abnormal masses ~ near antennae's field
Radiation amidst ~ the thyroid gland
To Earth's magnetics ~ Sun's emissions yield
Across death's spectrum ~ risky wavelengths spanned
That Faraday's cage ~ a laughable shield

  But ineffective ~ security regs[2]
  Let bandwidths (hawked ~ by humanity's dregs)
  Impinge cunningly ~ on defenseless eggs

Double-blind studies~ bares the corporate lie
Of diminished health ~ by straight statistic
Outside investors ~ smugly falsify
Say: *unbiased results ~ unrealistic*
Manufacturers ~ stay indemnified
Thru six font warnings ~ by sly linguistic

In fine legal print ~ of full disclosure
Advising *distance* ~ in your enclosure
Alluding to ~ indecent exposure

Ask Devra Davis ~ and Barrie Trower
Query the Bio- ~ Initiative
Indict the weapons-grade ~ bandwidth tower
On: *criminal acts, ~ disease-causative*
Blame the daily ~ frequency shower
For radiation, ~ cu-mu-lative

Capitalists remain ~ unmoved by pleas
To raise awareness ~ (asked by PhD's)
To reinstate ~ pollination to bees

Death waves marketed ~ with impunity
As creators stay ~ unapologetic
No serum offers ~ full immunity
To altered mito- ~ chondrial genetics
Data from the ~ IT community
At best, *confusing,* ~ worst, *synthetic*

Who, to laypersons, ~ they ever deny
Recorded hazards ~ to the nuclei
Yet their children's schools ~ prohibit Wi-Fi

Programmed search engines ~ slyly dismiss you
Sidetracking inquest ~ in off directions
And fertilizer ~ companies issue
Gaslights reasoning ~ for self-protection
But radiation ~ raids living tissue
Disrupting fetal ~ neural connections

Peer-reviewed studies ~ reveal disorders
From 5G dumped ~ on our sons and daughters
Like noxious fluoride ~ in healthy waters

And to the faithful ~ who curtsied and kneeled
Zealous petition ~ won't pray it away
A cache of weapons ~ offers not a shield
Forget protection ~ from the FDA
To green organics ~ wavelengths neither yield
Nor cock-eyed opti- ~ mism, allay

Helpless ova ~ (wholly unguarded)
By radiation ~ are bombarded
And fetal progress ~ may be retarded

Ralph Nader voiced ~ *consumer protection*
Gary Null marches ~ in a health crusade
CNN and Fox ~ in genuflection
To the globalists' ~ corrupt masquerade
And as tho' guilty ~ of insurrection
Assange is confined ~ dashing to truth's aid

Using positives like: ~ *FDA approved*
Unashamed phonies ~ continue unmoved
Knowing negatives ~ stay ever unproved

For farmers he attained ~ restitution
Thru principles and ~ honest lenity
And charged industry ~ with *wild pollution*
Indicted vaccine's ~ obscenity
For his father slain ~ sought no retribution
The honored junior ~ Robert Kennedy

  With injury rates ~ in rising percent
  They inoculate ~ mercuric offense
  At innocent children's ~ harmful expense

Agenda 21 ~ says you'll be bussed
To and from work ~ and all destinations
Sustainable growth ~ it commands *a must*
Redistricting water ~ (and other rations)
Corralling humans ~ is one of just
Imbedded guidelines ~ and false narrations

  Rosa Koire ~ encounters the task
  Answering questions ~ journalists won't ask
  In media like ~ *Behind the Green Mask*

Galloping nobly ~ to your salvation
The W-H-O ~ and C-D-C
Presenting counterfeit ~ arbitration
'Tween wireless gadgets ~ and mala-dy
Or sequestered facts ~ on vaccination
Awaiting visas ~ into you and me

  Dr. Alan Palmer's ~ *Truth Will Prevail*
  Twelve-hundred studies ~ as its holy grail
  Or Rima Laibow ~ on the serum trail

Try a single shot ~ of Willy's vaccine
Or a tempting bite ~ of Steve's Delicious
Autoimmunity ~ caused by squalene
Congenital faults ~ from waves malicious
Temptingly sweetened ~ by an altered gene
Or venomous apple ~ surreptitious

  Desire surrenders ~ to temptation's war
  T. Rex genuflects ~ to the meteor
  And Monsanto's seed ~ rots Eden's core

Masquerading poison ~ as *nutrients*
Misleading success ~ figures, falsified
Feed a child ~ vaccine's ingredients
You're imprisoned ~ makers indemnified
Capitalizing ~ on public nescience
But hidden injuries ~ VAERS identified

Those peddling harm ~ the machine protects
Insidious POPS ~ Codex resurrects
What's lawless to feed ~ big pharma injects

Scientists watching ~ how the trained behave
Especially mice ~ with skills acquired
Indecent exposure ~ to industry's wave
Only to have ~ their schooling bemired
As some of them met ~ a premature grave
Others' faculties ~ wholly retired

A flagrant case ~ of animal abuse
By the wanton filth ~ technicians induced
Now once-fertile mice ~ hardly reproduce

No dream of Kennedy's ~ or Eisenhower's
Promotes National ~ or Hitlerism
But one of history's ~ vomiting towers
Regurgitates ~ a solipsism:
As it merges state ~ and corporate powers
Fascism should be ~ called corporatism

  Multi-nationals' ~ narcissistic greed
  Grabbing all they want ~ as opposed to need
  Tycoons practicing ~ Mussolini's creed

Profusa employs ~ corporate nano-techs
To implant sensors ~ just below the skin
Or SARS two vaccine ~ hiding nano-flecks
Bonding evermore ~ to our cells within
DARPA's *Hydrogel* ~ with untried effects
To generate *end* ~ then here begin

  This is totalit- ~ arianism
  With thinking rooted ~ in Satanism
  And genesis of ~ transhumanism

Bodily functions ~ will be syncing
To online software ~ and a database
Private companies ~ will own your thinking
And upload memory ~ to hyperspace
New world supremacy ~ hijacks blinking
And nerve-endings in ~ your virtual face

  They'll stamp the time ~ and record position
  Analyze intent, ~ read disposition
  Then interrogate ~ all opposition

Joining the dots ~ of antiquity's tale
From thalidomide ~ to carcinogen
Agrichemicals ~ on a global scale
Toxaphene, chlordane, ~ and di-el-drin
Invasive hazards ~ Trade Agreements veil
From permitted poisons ~ to the mutagen

  Or Cutter's vaccine ~ to lead-laden paint
  Industry snubbing ~ the peoples' complaint
  On merchandise that's ~ all they claim it ain't

Typical to ~ Napoleonic Code
All that's unwritten ~ by default: *omitted*
Western tyranny ~ too manifes-toed
That risky compounds ~ go on permitted
Until damage is ~ "officially" showed
The products' guilt ~ remains acquitted

  Whether 5G waves ~ or a vaccine shot
  Both deemed innocent ~ 'til verified not
  If not attempted ~ transgression, then what?

Poe said: *Never ~ bet the devil your head*
Yet forests smolder ~ in purgatory
Super-consumers ~ leave millions unfed
While feasting on Earth's ~ fixed inventory
The petro-baron ~ (by gluttony led)
Turned our planet to ~ a crematory

  They forged Dante's hell ~ out of paradise
  Know *nothing's* value ~ but *everything's* price
  With offhand tosses ~ roll destiny's dice

An outlying stone ~ hosting life and granite
Or late-night horror ~ with insects teeming
Crawling creatures ~ try to run a planet
While its atmosphere ~ for air is screaming
Our species' agents ~ are Brad and Janet
Lost in time and space, ~ and empty meaning

 A science fiction ~ double showing
 To which theater buffs ~ keep movie-going
 And to caution's wind ~ (all reason) throwing

From time's beginning ~ 'til eighteen-o-one
One sightless family ~ slowly multiplies
A blind tribe running ~ in a race un-won
Sapiens barely ~ reach two-billion thighs
With just two hundred ~ more tours around Sun
Dwellers still can't see ~ thru sixteen-billion eyes

 To bottom in ~ a suicidal race
 In just two centuries ~ at the human pace
 Seven billion more ~ wear the human face

Ovaries perversely ~ spermatocized
By suicidal ~ curiosity
Misogyny's spying ~ waves womanized
As prying currents ~ breed monstrosity
History's futurists ~ go on unsurprised
While plutocrats warp ~ human zygosity

Into woman's eggs ~ greed's frequency nosed
To deformity ~ ever predisposed
And obscenity's wave ~ ova-exposed

Finis

1. Eric Arthur Blair was better known by his pen name, George Orwell
2. Short for *regulations*

Ink from History's Bottle

There are those who say ~ I should remodel
Victorian themes ~ spoken yesteryear
By dispensing words ~ from history's bottle
And updating verse ~ for the trendy ear
Or drawing from Yeats ~ and Aristotle
Then bill myself ~ as a new sonneteer

So love tales emerge ~ with refreshing slants
And lyrics adorn ~ Gregorian chants
By creative ink ~ my feather decants

I'd alter slapstick ~ into myst-er-y
Recast Poe's thrillers ~ with new persona
Streamline narratives ~ throughout hist-or-y
And move a comedy ~ from *Verona*
Then alter its theme ~ into witchery
And bill it: *Two Wizards ~ of Savona*

Redrafting humor ~ leaving play-goers tense
So the caption reads: ~ *William's New Suspense*
In blood-curdling ink ~ shrewdly dispensed

Quantum Narratives

My pen reconstructs ~ antique paragraphs
Into an array ~ of modern stories
Tipping more fluid ~ from olden carafes
To quill notes on ~ divine allegories
Affording readers ~ uproarious laughs
When proving fraud in ~ Dante's purgatories

Then win the award ~ in the Poet's Guild
For the presentation ~ frankly distilled
By the comedic ~ truthful ink I spilled

Finis

Benjamin Vaccaro

Joey and Her Jax

One young daybreak ~ over Rue de St. Mark's
Where destiny's eye ~ is closely viewing
'Neath the melodies ~ of rose-colored larks
Stands the dark-light form ~ of Jax debuting
The poignant theme ~ of the rhyme ensuing

  The climbing Sun loses ~ its shy-red face
  Illuminating ~ Jax's shining grace

Darkness bids farewell ~ to night's zodi-ac
As dewdrops condense ~ on a cobwebbed morn
Court-jestering Jax ~ contrasts white to black
Like Cancer's tropic ~ to its Capricorn
Or crystalline salt ~ the peppercorn

  Tho' morning moisture, ~ Sun vaporizes
  Jax's handsome air ~ *beauty* idolizes

Prancing and stopping ~ thru the emerald fields
To unknown movement, ~ posts rapt fixation.
And to unnamed sound ~ Jax cautiously yields
Staying keenly fixed ~ (pending affirmation)
And warning compass ~ confirms location

  With judicious ear ~ and watchful glances
  He surveys the field ~ reducing chances

Pledging face-to-face ~ their love undying
Joey and her Jax ~ in meditation
The mutual stare ~ that each was eying
As tho' sensing ~ the other's vibration
Seers decrypting ~ unsaid narrations

 Jocularity ~ proximity sprung
 Reciprocal pecks ~ from pursed lips flung

Squarely up and down ~ with vertical poise
Bipedal (at times) ~ but treads most on four
Behind, on both mitts, ~ Jax often enjoys
A two-pawed waltz ~ on a circular tour
In whichever direction ~ either/or

 Non-stop orbits~ (more laps, the merrier)
 A cork-screwed marvel, ~ Jax, the terrier

Of *Jaxie-Boy, Batman,* ~ and *Cracker-Jax*
To announce a few ~ of several nicknames
Forceful loins wherein ~ authority packs
To cheerfully play ~ in innocent games
When pacing on two ~ he (the humankind) feigns

 Chessboard dominance ~ pre-calculating
 Checkmating doubt ~ of the speculating

With her two-toned boy ~ no semblance agrees
More than those bearing ~ the proudest of sight
Pelt juxtaposed, ~ like dissimilar keys
Or notes of grand worth ~ sweetly up-right
Piano'd likeness, ~ as ebon to white

  Joey's song of flats, ~ naturals, and sharps
  Plucking rhapsodies ~ on Cupid-like harps

Priceless appraisal ~ values his estate
Ears pricked, eyes keen, ~ and a dew-laden nose
The discerning eye ~ fails to overrate
Justice Jax offers ~ to the civil rose
Or ballerinas ~ arabesque'd in pose

  His développé dares ~ posing avocets
  Plumb revolutions, ~ Gelsey's[1] pirouettes

Thru a cage of ribs ~ unfailing strengths course
With muscles sporting ~ vascularity
Distinguished carriage ~ like a regal horse
Conveying tales ~ with focused clarity
And victories using ~ muscularity

  Neither poise (such ~ ascendancy) excludes
  Nor errand from governance ~ his might precludes

Happily wild, ~ in frisky passion,
Upright on two ~ (rising from all fours)
Offer your palms ~ (in pat-a-cake fashion)
Tapping, he replies, ~ with childlike paws
Letting his front mitts ~ to collide with yours

  As other canines ~ compete with swaying
  From ninety degrees ~ he's not a-straying

Bouncily greeting you ~ on a bubbly spree
Jax wears steadiness ~ in right precision
Upon admission ~ he charges a fee
In cadenced phrases ~ of spright concision
Friendly fringes ~ in social collision

  His entrance duty ~ (like a joint applause)
  Remit two palms ~ he'll return two paws

Non-fictional eyes ~ you can believeth
Circular crystals ~ reflect honest themes
Faceted phrases ~ from Jax's zenith
Articulating ~ the beauty he means
As porcelain splendor ~ in figurines

  Or honeysweet grape ~ of the Gamay vine
  And Venus's glow ~ advertising shine

Due south of the eyes ~ misty portals flare
Reverberating ~ thru a morning snooze
Sensing the moisture ~ of heart-heated air
Two tropical gusts ~ from two nostrils ooze
And then the cutest ~ occurrence ensues

  Joey, face-to-face ~ lounges opposing
  Teasingly she ~ and Jax sit-a-nosing

He's a pageant of ~ ordered refinements
And legend penned ~ by the biographer
A drafted plan ~ of clever alignments
And map detailed ~ by a cartographer
Or lavish symbol, ~ the calligrapher

  And powerhouse of ~ nimble fortitude
  Modeling graceful ~ lines of latitude

His airborne gallop ~ as tho' suspended
Like the stainless grace ~ of a sprinting steed
Or competing hound ~ with limbs extended
Of excess finesse, ~ Jax is in no need
Bostonian poise ~ of a stately breed

  As goes the gemstone ~ proficiently set
  Garb unblemished ~ of a navy cadet

Approximating ~ a grey-scaled twister
Pepper and salt ~ blots a soccer-ball head
Impersonating ~ a fumbling sister
As glory to the ~ nun's homily said:
Poppy seeds season ~ our daily bread

  A habited treat ~ garbed in dark and light
  Or sistered monochrome ~ where black joins white

Bi-folded upward ~ and well-appointed
Two velvet facets ~ roost atop the gem
Out-sizing their host, ~ pricked and disjointed
Furry funnels therefrom ~ gracefully stem
What laughter to waft ~ in either of them

  Past *Batman* reference ~ (in particular)
  Sprout ears, from this jewel, ~ perpendicular

Nuzzled with Jo-Jo, ~ rescheduling time
Like a warm sector ~ where hatchlings nest
When resonating ~ a familiar rhyme
He unlocks his eyes ~ then returns to rest
'Neath the binary care ~ of gentle breasts

  Her arms, his chamber, ~ and bosom, his bed
  In safe asylum ~ cribs a napping head

One dusky moment ~ of late-noon dreaming
A bluish image ~ to Miss Joey showed
Uninvited yet ~ forcefully streaming
Its fullest import ~ she could not decode
Is time's itinerant ~ at a forked road?

 Redrafting themes ~ in life's first edition
 Rethinking soundness ~ of superstition

With the aura blue ~ (softly) vignetting
Evening plays witness ~ to her grave unease
But blueness blackened ~ to silhouetting
As fear blew in ~ on mortality's breeze
Propelling Jo-Jo's ~ disquieting pleas

 Haunting imagery ~ steadily theming
 She frightfully asks, ~ "Is karma scheming?"

A hapless sky ~ (given its assignment)
Of a cheerless tale ~ lying in wait
The agenda in ~ the stars' alignment
Foreshows the journey ~ of a cherished mate
And itinerary ~ of his estate

 Sir Jax, the two-year gift, ~ destiny brings
 On a fate-sealed crossing ~ where angels sing

Complex arrangement, ~ entropy destroys
Egyptian pyramids, ~ at last, decay
Falling satellites ~ NASA re-deploys
But gravity will ~ (every atom) slay
A ceaseless order, ~ cosmologists say

  The dropped heirloom seed ~ employs its duty
  Seasonal rebirth ~ thru time takes beauty

Next morn finds Jax ~ thru a window peering
A leashed companion ~ wins his attention
His urge to frolic ~ too domineering
And *might* overcame ~ a screen-door's tension
Life's pre-unwritten lease ~ revoked extension

  Playfully offering ~ a passionate scratch
  Where death's door hinges ~ on a ten-cent latch

Two contrasting things, ~ for equal space, vie
One from nature, ~ a second, Detroit's hand
The former priceless, ~ latter, monies buy
As a fairytale, ~ say, to Disneyland
Or pianist (skilled) ~ the seven-foot grand

  Pauli's electrons ~ with similar spin
  Excludes all kingdoms ~ quantum life lives in

A front-page newsflash ~ for which no one braced
Or as fate penned it: ~ *perhaps, just because*
Where industry's steel ~ (guiltless flesh) displaced
Four vulcanized rounds ~ engage fleshy fours
The bulletin reads: ~ *Wheels Overtake Paws*

  Cinderella's coach ~ beyond a deadline
  Unhappier still ~ the current headline

Amazing Grace chants ~ by a soprano
And distant chimes ~ in the grey of noon
There, in the street, ~ Joey's pieced piano
With all patterned keys ~ no longer in tune
On a nearby church ~ two steepled bells croon

  A loving doggie ~ unfailingly tame
  Celestial Jax ~ whom the angels name

No self-centered registrant, ~ hitherto
Grieves his stock-still van ~ with a dented grille
More than a vilomah[2] ~ with the ghastly view
Of his stock-still pet ~ lying mutely still
Thru Sire's spine spread ~ mortality's chill

  Identifying ~ all wounds internal
  Sire revises ~ fate's cheery journal

Lawn ornaments in ~ astonishment stood
Curious neighbors ~ in horror, appraised
Willows seen weeping ~ doubted likelihood
An aimless driver ~ grotesquely unfazed
Then by Sire's arms ~ loving Jax was raised

A human auto ~ on a dark journey
Two legs playing hearse ~ two arms, a gurney

On nearby greens ~ wherein nasal passage
Sire tries reviving ~ with makeshift care
He thrusts Jax's chest ~ with loving massage
Then his sky-bound fists ~ lobbies it to spare
Oh! The useless attempt ~ of sire-forced air

But the glacial sky ~ gave no salvation
Sire's drive iced up ~ at resuscitation

To a standstill screeched ~ bicycled kiddies
Whilst a squirrel chipped ~ a sorrowful tune
High-wired sparrows ~ chirped mournful ditties
Two storm-drained possums ~ unhappily croon
Yet to each other ~ refused to commune

A stranger's attempt ~ at consoling words
Was plagiarized by ~ hovering birds

Sire, by now ~ all but reconciled
Fate's arbiter ~ unjustly refereed
Lady Capulet mourned ~ her self-stabbed child
Lord Montague to ~ woe's poison concedes
With fate's magistrate ~ Sire disagreed

  On short verdant blades ~ freshly trim and groomed
  Lay motionless Jax ~ briefly a-tombed

How to publish ~ this event, depressing
Sire calls Jo-Jo ~ in the not-too-distance
Words strangled him, ~ thus forsook addressing
But *terror* seeped thru ~ his choked resistance
Joey shrieks, "What life ~ left this existence?"

  Never thinking Jaxie ~ could be the prey
  Unconscious she fell ~ hearing Sire say

Her later entrance ~ (in hollow pursuit)
Mourns once-vibrant life ~ too-soon truncated
Like Venus's shift, ~ from wax to wane transmute
Or Moon's eighth house, ~ by and by vacated
And the vowel-less word, ~ abbreviated

  Ten centuries holler~ the Redwood's story
  Just sixty-minutes ~ the Morning Glory

                                                Benjamin Vaccaro

Fresh salinity ~ encrusts Joey's cheeks
Her blue panes blacken ~ by the death they saw
Barren striations ~ like white banded streaks
Etch sorrow about ~ her quivering jaw
Asking destiny, ~ "Why the shortest straw"

  Kneeling o'er his body ~ she touched his ears
  And spattered his pelt ~ with plummeting tears

On his taut-skinned fleece ~ of ivory and black
A nocturne drips ~ in C-sharp minor third
Neither moonlight did ~ her sonata lack
Nor ever there was ~ more passion bestirred
Than by wistful notes ~ or funerary word

  While knelt and sobbing ~ o'er her pet reposed,
  Rains an unplanned opus ~ (on him composed)

Joey's tears darken ~ all nature's beauty
Her hard-working heart ~ lingers unemployed
Honoring Jax ~ with musical duty
She sings a coda ~ he always enjoyed
Chanting the ode: ~ *I love thee Jaxie Boy*

  With deepening woe ~ throughout deliverance
  Atonal phrases ~ rasp in dissonance

Salt-caked traces, ~ from dropt tears, remain
And stripes Jax's hide ~ so to streak it white
Zebraic likeness ~ his countenance feigns
As the waxing gibbous ~ contrasts the night
Or considerate, ~ bouts the impolite

  Soiled hands, scuffed knees, ~ and hearts twice vexed
  Enduring grief rules ~ the proceeding next:

Leans o'er his boy ~ for a stately raise
King Jax (to chest height) ~ is elevated
Into his eyes ~ Sire loans love's gaze
As the fallen king ~ remained checkmated
With all life's forces ~ unanimated

  In death, a czar ~ retains nobility
  Tho' a cureless mass ~ of immobility

In measured movement, ~ barely walking
Unaccompanied ~ in their procession
Unspeakable grief ~ (just silence talking)
Taking languid steps ~ in sad succession
Sire's tender prize ~ in his arms' possession

  Both limbs engaged ~ (Joey opens death's door)
  Sire places Jax ~ on a wooden floor

Joey and Her Jax

Joey's eyes survey ~ Jax's, with yearning
His lifeless features ~ ever waxing clear
Her two lamps glowing ~ (as his once burning)
She (much) cries his name ~ he (more) cannot hear
Nor was Jax aware ~ of Joey's dropt tear

  Inactive below ~ and Joey above
  Lay motionless life ~ drizzled in love

A handkerchief clothes ~ Jo-jo's wrist and hand
With the snuggest fit ~ like a uniform
Embroidered thereon ~ (with eloquent strands)
Astute embossments ~ assume human form
And calligraphies ~ stitched in cuneiform

  Into which there was ~ ancient wisdom hemmed
  Spelling out clearly: ~ *all here are condemned*

The lead figure tends ~ to persistent sobs
A second muses ~ on mortality
A third is wrinkled ~ by repeated swabs
But all understand ~ causality,
Alpha, omega, ~ and finality

  The team manages ~ Joey's weeping orbs
  As one saturates ~ its backup absorbs

Thru liquescent eyes ~ at the floor she stares
With comprehension ~ of maple, straight-grained
To which (in a flash) ~ wordlessly compares
Jax's striated loins ~ with eyes so trained
And lengthened muscles ~ attractively veined

  Her shivering lips ~ signal her wrecked tongue
  And choked, she stutters, ~ "He-he died so young"

Resembling a sun- ~ soaked flower petal
Beauty unchallenged ~ sweet beyond appraise
Tho' salty tears rust ~ the blacksmith's metal
Thru costly heartache ~ Joey's grace conveys
The edicts of sorrow ~ she disobeys

  'Neath bloodshot eyes ~ (like oxidized cherries)
  Decorum's tongue ~ rhetorically queries:

Why called upon me ~ has this woeful day,
Where an unseen force ~ wrecked future design
That I presupposed ~ Jax's lengthened stay
Or have short-lived love ~ just slain in its prime?
"I concur," Sire wails, ~ "'Twas not his time."

Since times of yore ~ and many things anew
Little continues ~ worthy of her view

Benjamin Vaccaro

A naïve seamstress ~ dreaming to unweave
And unknit this tale ~ (in desperate quest)
Joey muses when ~ Jax would neatly sleeve
And braid himself ~ in her protective breast
So she enfolds him ~ for a final rest

  Internal damage ~ her fingertips felt
  Thru the lousy hand ~ fate's dealer misdealt

Sympathetic pain ~ leaves her close-fisted
As in, finally set ~ harsh reality
Vexing Joey's soul ~ by fate so twisted
She ponders canine ~ immortality
Then deliberates ~ all legality

  Unbalanced by Jax's ~ gross inversions
  To justice's scale ~ argues: *Subversion*

Charging the powers ~ with highest treason
And fraudulent acts ~ of life's contract breached
Neither heart nor mind ~ tendered just reason
For the unjust ruling ~ fate's jurors reached
To a grinding halt ~ wheels of justice screeched

  Righteousness triumphs ~ had *honor* been its
  Sole magistrate ~ of the trial's minutes

Gravity's empire ~ notwithstanding
And ephemeral life ~ time's overthrown
Transient heavens ~ ever-expanding
(Two one-way contracts ~ binding and foreknown)
By embossments in ~ Jo-jo's hankie (sewn)

  Before the cosmos ~ undergo collapse
  Hubble contended ~ *expansion* perhaps

And Jax was skillful ~ in aerobatics
Splendor presented ~ no competition
Balletic contours ~ graced mathematics
Choreographed by ~ a geometrician
But time minus-ed ~ its only addition

  Flowing symmetries ~ of Euclidean grace
  Adding majesty ~ to 3D space

When filtering thru ~ her archived annals
Joey finds a few ~ then reminisces
Charming occasions ~ her broke heart channels
Of the honeyed times ~ her broke heart misses
From his bouncy romp ~ to bartered kisses

  A brief adjournment ~ from endless sorrows
  Three sweet abridgements ~ from history borrows:

***

He'd forcibly discharge ~ a humid breeze
A nasal tempest ~ of tropical mist
But greeted by ~ Jax's lovable sneeze
Like a garden hose ~ that buoyantly spritzed
Of this occasions ~ Joey reminisced

  Indexed memoirs ~ by his human mother
  Bring bittersweet thoughts ~ then cites another:

Four bunched paws in ~ napping consultation
'Tween fleshy cushions ~ peek feathery fringe
As she tickled his ~ clumped congregation
She laughed, he snoozed, ~ as they'd comically twinge
Four quivering mitts ~ yon their ankles' hinge

  During the folly ~ he'd sometimes waken
  Seeing her, returned ~ to sleep unshaken

The drawn breath supplies ~ his chest a-swelling
Joey's cheek to Jax, ~ on her side, she lies
Resting her head ~ for so brief a dwelling
Ogling marvels ~ of undulant skies
With little distress ~ over *hows* and *whys*

  The last reflection ~ of her cherished friend
  Reality brings ~ the trilogy's end

***

Abjuration speaks ~ a second appeal
On narrowing grounds ~ solicits the claim
To the broken spokes ~ on destiny's wheel
She cross-examines: ~ *what (of him) became*
And meanings specific ~ to Jax's name

  Unyielding sadness ~ fuels more denial
  Thru weakened protest ~ pursues mistrial

Dodging the process ~ of *discovery*
The opposition ~ slips in an instrument
For damages, Joey ~ seeks recovery
And subpoenas court ~ for the document
To search for any ~ winning argument

  Reviewing the writ ~ then stricken solemn
  Finding Jax indexed ~ in the Obit column

The gaveled verdict ~ stays undisputed
Ethereal jurors ~ hear no petition
Joey's argument ~ misfortune muted
Succumbing to no ~ right of rescission
A final edit ~ of its sole edition

  As destiny's bench ~ firmly countermands
  Jo-Jo collapses, ~ but the judgement stands

Enlightened Buddhists ~ process misery
Knowing human grief ~ feeds on earthly ties
Life's impermanence ~ (unrescissory)
'Gainst which no tonic ~ can anesthetize
Top Secrets of change ~ death declassifies

From sweet attachment ~ sentients suffer
Sour detachment ~ no physic buffers

Flowerbeds blossom ~ 'neath Joey's smiles
Gardens decompose ~ under tears of grief
Her energy sprouts ~ green juveniles
Her wisdom accepts ~ the autumnal leaf
And canine hourglass ~ however brief

The planter wherein ~ purple asters bloom
Serves every need from ~ basinet to tomb

In a deep-state dream ~ one deserted night
Petitioning Jax ~ thru blustery sighs
Joey slurs, "Have you ~ seen hereafter's light?"
Left unrequited ~ kisses him good-bye
As morn's rose wakens ~ Jax evermore flies

Never mortal tongue ~ thru slumbering word
Reached departed ear ~ of life interred

Like a stately czar ~ promoting splendor
Wherein the posture ~ perched a striking head
And naïve methods ~ (routinely tender)
Olympian leaps ~ held a six-foot spread
With no delusion ~ now ever lies dead

 King Jax paraded ~ once upon St. Mark's
 Ever silence reigns ~ thus nevermore barks

Finis

1. Gelsey Kirkland was an illustrious Prima Ballerina for
    American Ballet Theater
2. Vilomah – Sanskrit for parent of a deceased child

Memo in the Sand

Prologue

The astral playwright ~ of this eve's theater
Casts her and him, ~ a coastline, and tide
Whereon virgin shores ~ twilight premiered her
Only to himself ~ and no one besides
Like a back-stage pass ~ *all access* implied

The venue is ~ an outdoor arena
Where *love at first sight* ~ tells the story line
Mythical spirits ~ bestow patina
On only two roles ~ the heavens assign
Beamed from Venus ~ to human from divine

But the closing script ~ memo-ed in the sand
Streams love by water ~ to deep sea from land

***

One mystical twilight ~ I halted rowing
'Cross the wrinkled skin ~ of a poignant sea
'Neath perceptive eyes ~ (as tho' foreknowing)
The universe wakes ~ up from dormancy
As self-aware stars ~ pledge transiency

In their alignment ~ flickers a story
With a subtext couched ~ in mysticism
Or Greco-Roman ~ allegory
Replete with themes ~ of eroticism
Seductively beamed ~ thru euphemism

Horizontal oars ~ drip water, like rain
As I mind forecasts ~ from fate's weather vane

Foamed, from an ocean ~ love's epic daughter
As Uranus suffered ~ genital shearing
Deity Venus ~ arose from water
While destiny's wind ~ takes over steering
And unknown to me ~ toward beauty nearing

Like gravity or ~ unseen magnetics
Intangible force ~ acts upon my craft
Heavenly dances ~ (in lithe balletics)
Twinkle sneak previews ~ fate choreographed
With extra backing ~ from a cryptic draft

Sailed into a trance ~ on seawater tame
With navigation ~ toward an ocean frame

Struggling with ~ diminishing light
Wherefrom two bare knees ~ I begin to rise
Broken coastlines ~ emerge from night
But one expressly ~ *nearness* clarifies
Mending breaks by passion ~ and two fixed eyes

There a private shore ~ hosts a silent form
Owning well-scaled curves ~ and sinuous themes
Diaphanous silk ~ is its uniform
As a naked face ~ blazed radiant beams
In a sandy cove ~ wherefrom honey streams

  Fate's captain rudders ~ with predestined aim
  Like a spellbound moth ~ drawn to peerless flame

A storybook tide ~ yaws me into the loch
Skippers my vessel ~ with a guiding hand
A shell-scattered beach ~ gives no place to dock
But for a leafless bank ~ of sea-washed sand
Near the soundless form ~ from a dreamy land

'Neath stars confessing ~ a cosmic mission
I'm wordlessly questioned ~ by a nubile
Dream that placed me ~ under love's suspicion
(As well as oath) ~ by her undone smile
Shared testimonies ~ in a speechless trial

  Neither silent guise ~ heighten the twain
  Nor signed affidavit ~ more ascertain

Trafficking *beauty* ~ across dwindling space
Four eyes (in contract) ~ trade passionate stares
Mediating looks ~ 'tween my sight, her face
Where milk-white features ~ vend prettified wares
As a peacock hawks ~ the spectrum it bears

Her stillness campaigns ~ vanishing twilight
To nominate night's ~ deep blue complexion
And chaperons time ~ far beyond midnight
To later cast votes ~ for Sun's resurrection
Or ballot for dawn's ~ young re-election

Disembarking there ~ petitioned her name
Yet, without reply ~ she and I became

I tossed a blanket ~ on the sandy ground
Where we establish ~ a makeshift dwelling
Childish tensions ~ ostensibly drowned
Deep in the legend ~ her eyes are telling
As a treasure sunk ~ 'neath ocean's swelling

Our quilt inhabits ~ shy embroidered forms
With reticent cheeks ~ and self-conscious eyes
The shapes are summoned ~ to surrender norms
(Like prissiness and ~ Victorian guise)
And watch us vacate ~ bans on night's nude skies

'Neath the wingspread of ~ oceanic cranes
One nosy form urged, ~ "Please tell us your names"

Discourse amongst ~ two rivulets gushing
Infect us with ~ acute mesmerism
Thru moon-lit shadows ~ peek hints of blushing
As mimicking streams ~ do plagiarism
For all attraction ~ blame magnetism

Crosswinds pairing ~ in one vicinity
Where common vapors ~ hotly coexist
Around my portal's ~ shared proximity
She introduces ~ combustible mist
From Cupid's red bow ~ heretofore un-kissed

  If a tongue be art ~ and lips the frame
  The signature then ~ is a kiss-ed name

Torsos engaged ~ in mutual leaning
As predisposed frames ~ willingly align
To communicate ~ nonverbal meaning
In an unknown tongue ~ of the lovers' kind
In miscible gasses ~ passion combined

Should kissing hold tints ~ it would don all shades
Owning flavor, ~ release the tang of love
And if touchable ~ feel like silken suedes
Or aromatic ~ the sweet-scented dove
But if flammable ~ then all the above

  After the breath ~ yet before the flame
  Sociable ethers ~ gather 'twixt the twain

Time (all around us) ~ lost identity
Destiny's timepiece ~ rescheduled ticks
Reason struggled ~ to halve infinity
Volcanoes erupt ~ when our rims affix
And hot-blooded outbreaths ~ fiercely intermix

A wet tongue traces ~ a crimson ellipse
Like a breathing portrait ~ outlining its frame
Steadily coursing ~ charting lips toward lips
Thru explosive gas ~ to ignite love's flame
As two sketches joined, ~ one art, became

  Swapping steamy drafts ~ merging frame to frame
  White-hot passion ~ burst red into flame

Like two peninsulas ~ colliding in night
With dripping wet banks ~ of a three-shored beach
Itinerant tongues ~ (in thirst, unite)
Plainly imbibing ~ the language of each
Swapping dialect ~ thru the freest speech

Both identify ~ French vernacular
Upholding France's ~ breathy exhalations
As the rolling tongue ~ trills alveolar
Lingual peninsulas ~ trade phonation
In wordless parlance ~ needing no translation

  Subducting masses ~ slide plane over plane
  Bordered by better ~ froth than French champagne

Love's thirst (I suppose) ~ quenches us at length
Sirius above ~ brightly luminesced
Perhaps lust (not love) ~ over us wields strength
Then by readiness ~ maiden veils divest
Introducing night ~ to heavenly guests

Making a debut ~ as twins fraternal
Goddesses casting ~ double avatars
Unequal features ~ gracefully vernal
Like opening flickers ~ from nursling stars
Or Isis's shine ~ extracted from Ra

 Astronomic links ~ by an unseen chain
 To heaven's suns and ~ Earth's, each appertain

Alabaster worlds ~ spotlighting darkness
As a risen curtain ~ on a play's premiere
Beauty's two fables ~ (in total starkness)
Obliging modesty ~ to disappear
Exposing truth ~ (forcing mistiness clear)

Hither and thither ~ lose all composure
Former asks latter ~ in naked wonder
Celestial forms ~ give full disclosure
To a crescent eye ~ eying what's under
As a high-noon star ~ fancied it sunned her

 Magnificence to ~ strike the agile lame
 Adding black to night ~ deeper red to flame

Two earthly sisters ~ share a parable
With ancient brethren ~ thru boundless distance
Flashing twin fables ~ (incomparable)
Of beauteous forms ~ in co-existence
And mirrored splendor ~ in equidistance

Remote equals comb ~ the vacuum of space
Like astronomers with ~ curiosity
For lineage (they) ~ of any trace
(Or echoes of ~ reciprocity)
Receive albedos ~ of luminosity

Thru all-seeing eyes ~ with infinite aim
Star to star they find ~ likenesses, the same

Sir Isaac proposed ~ an analogy:
Attraction relates ~ to gravitation
Assume we employ ~ astrology
(With perfect contour ~ and separation)
Then two stars entice ~ in constellation

Arousing wavelengths ~ nameless to humans
One star glistens ~ erotic color
Another bursting ~ infinite lumens
In like frequencies ~ (no less duller)
Unveiled just to gods ~ and twilit sculler

Mythical deities ~ fight to contain
Earthly desire ~ to caress the twain

Between our heartbeats ~ there was little break
Thru my extremities ~ dry sand sifted
One hand performing ~ as a five-tined rake
The other whose ~ priority shifted
Toward topographies ~ faultlessly rifted

Constitution set ~ my fingers adrift
As a neckline ebbs ~ like receding tides
To a hill-flanked gulf ~ cleaved by astral gifts
Or Binary Stars* ~ that heaven divides
'Tween two risen worlds, ~ ecstasy resides

  Celestial bodies ~ in an earthly game
  On *heavenly guests* ~ astronomers blame

Negotiating ~ regional valleys
Finding passage 'round ~ anonymous curves
Secrecies keeping ~ seductive alleys
Thru which my tracing ~ curiously swerves
And uniquely ~ night's crescent observes

Hot winds kick up ~ in breath-like spasms
Or stimulating ~ intermittent gales
Symmetries riven ~ by perfect chasms
Arboreal knolls ~ fringe a private dale
All fantasies by ~ comparison pale

  Instructing high Moon ~ from Earth's terrain
  And stellular guides: ~ *ever wax not wane*

One embroidered form ~ spoke literary
Another became ~ voyeuristic
A few more eavesdropped ~ on commentary
All assimilate ~ the French linguistic
Recounting us in ~ the euphemistic:

To a fabled night ~ played aural witness
Felt infrared warmth ~ ooze from two physiques
Matured watching youth ~ flex lingual fitness
Observed passion flare ~ thru meddlesome peeks
Which heretofore ~ rubified our cheeks

Blanketed bodies ~ (heat) always retain
Here youth warms blankets ~ by overlain

It's as tho' fate wrote ~ night a unplanned book
With a plot needing ~ no explanation
Some pictures demanded ~ a second look
Others left little ~ to imagination
Exposed neatly ~ by shrewd pagination

Headlining as ~ a best-selling story
Possessing themes ~ of a sensual tale
For bookworms, its read ~ is mandatory
With textured pages ~ for those knowing braille
And all embossments ~ proportioned to scale

The published draft ~ owns critical acclaim
But I scanned chapters ~ fate has yet to name

Benjamin Vaccaro

A veteran shore ~ sips ongoing floods
As her eyes reflect ~ evening's lunar dance
Along water's edge ~ ferment brimming suds
Brewing two night-birds ~ into one sweet trance
To horizon's craft ~ (glow) a lighthouse grants

Self-discipline sinks ~ deep in midnight's sea
As love unmoors ~ near a poignant ocean
Starriest eyes ~ anesthetize me
Paralyzing will, ~ impairing motion
As tho' needled with ~ love's honeyed potion

 An astral elixir ~ from another plane
 I dreamt a sand-castle ~ wherein we reign

***

The castle's acreage ~ (in my reflection)
Holds magical brooks ~ coursing thru the wild
Transient birds ~ lose sense of direction
And unsolved footpaths ~ mystify a child
In flowerbeds trim ~ mums domiciled

'Twould route thru gardens ~ of fruit forbidden
Like a nosy foal ~ in virgin for-es-try
A trail for my stagecoach ~ (both un-ridden)
Or nomadic stitch ~ thru a ta-pes-try
Of woven tales from ~ bygone an-ces-try

 Whilst other traits roar ~ of soaring pillars
 Inside lions wait ~ blamed, dungeon'd killers
           Or a maiden stitch ~ thru a ta-pes-try

The outer stratum ~ is alabaster skinned
And the lower berth ~ moors a one-man craft
Around two Turrets ~ whips a churning wind
As the Bailey pants ~ love's balmiest draft
But for my presence ~ would remain unstaffed

The vacant fortress ~ recites stairs of jewels
Matchless charm to tempt ~ a vile prowler
I'd hone my blade ~ for passionate duels
And safeguard the queen's ~ unsullied flower
Then lastly sharpen ~ the dullest hour

  Polishing skin ~ of alabaster
  Chafing other things ~ even faster

Its floorplan mirrors ~ persuasive designs
Laying claim to ~ Elizabethan style
Flanking trellises ~ of manicured vines
Heightens admittance ~ to a central aisle
Or as pink-red lips ~ upgrades the smile

Suspending flora ~ (slinging symmetric)
Like an upturned pair ~ of butterfly wings
Narrow halls curtained ~ (stereometric)
Here a stately pair ~ have secretive flings
Ecstasy for queens, ~ euphoria, kings

  Freshly shorn gardens ~ in Flemish shapes
  Of ripened fruit where ~ the visceral traipse

The fort is cast ~ from indigenous grains
Like powdered sugar ~ or cottony bales
Atop two towers ~ point two weather vanes
Toward arousing winds ~ that arouse our sails
Dictating showers ~ preaching steamy tales

Provocative drafts ~ tease the ocean's crust
As it tailors sand ~ evenly rippled
Protruding whitecaps ~ from a tempting gust
Like Venetian plaster ~ sublimely stippled
Or breath-teased breast ~ erotically nipple'd

  Ingression to ~ the sanctified palace
  Here, a Pagan's blade ~ transects a chalice

Inside the queen's court ~ (as a stationed guard)
I'd wield a potent ~ sentient sword
So firm a blade sheathed ~ by so sweet a yard
As a ready skiff ~ in a willing fjord
Or harbored kayak ~ ecstatically moored

At crowning times, ~ the castle floods its moat
Apprehending me ~ inside stately walls
I'd scale high Turrets ~ o'er my tethered boat
And populate daily ~ its un-walked halls
Protecting craft (and me) ~ from violent squalls

  I'd tell the queen: ~ *there are more stars than grains*
  Whilst heavenly guests ~ fuel devilish veins

Charmed cargo anchored ~ in the lower hold
From bow to stern ~ deck hands navigated
Oars of wooden ore – trimmed in flesh-toned gold
Like valueless tin ~ Rhodium plated
Or low-priced vessel ~ Gold capsulated

Exquisite fingers ~ form new-sprung metals
Rowing me away ~ from ebbing boy-age
Her palms held texture ~ (as gilded petals)
Forging with my ore ~ lustful alloy-age
Like a virgin jaunt ~ or maiden voyage

  At cresting wave height ~ all deck hands added
  Stroking precious oars ~ which her gold cladd-ed

The echo within ~ marble corridors
Reverberates cries ~ of a ruling queen
The Dungeon resounded ~ lion-like roars
As minstrels plucked lutes ~ from the Mezzanine
And the Lady's Bower ~ remained unseen

I'd enter the Chapel ~ in great respect
Then comb the Pantry ~ in sweet appetite
Plunder the Bottlery ~ when left unchecked
And breach the Gatehouse ~ with increased delight
But most (the Great Hall) ~ there I'd waltz each night

  In morn, I'd waken ~ alongside a queen
  And describe a view ~ from a sultry dream:

I heard untamed breaths ~ imitating breeze
Saw carnal reflections ~ in burnished strands
I whiffed ocean brine ~ of bordering seas
Sprayed the mist of love ~ across honeyed lands
And in courtyards which ~ just by me, were manned

I know the castle ~ held antiquity
I sensed yesterdays ~ etched into its stone
Ever echoing ~ past activity
Of a coupled queen ~ coupled on a throne
To only me ~ and only me alone

I was naïve ~ yet boyishly vital
You, a castle, who ~ o'er me held title

There were echoed moans ~ of one syllable
Eagerly gasping ~ alliteration
Feral appetites ~ hardly fillable
Hotly exhaling ~ reiteration
In accents needing ~ fierce punctuation

Pleasure gave rise ~ to a corollary
In monophonic ~ desirous yowls
But with restricted ~ vocabulary
And repetition ~ of sensual howls
I heard you panting ~ erogenous vowels

By divested bra ~ you unveiled to stars
Pressing night on me ~ iterating "aaahs"

***

A salty breeze sprays ~ a torrid story
Of unchecked desire ~ (above refute)
On love-struck sand ~ steams an allegory
Of a young man's roar ~ when yesterday mute
Could alchemy's lead ~ into gold transmute?

Prosecution from ~ undulating waves
We counter-sue with ~ love's euphoric moan
Her nomadic touch ~ (to fathoms) engraves
Cupid's missive ~ in powdery stone
Or littoral sand ~ (by heaven, foreknown)

  With an orphaned twig ~ she composed my name
  Channeling Venus ~ hoping I, the same

If a fleck of sand ~ equals *impassioned*
Then I'll compose ~ a rhapsody of grains
Drawing from shoreline ~ (cleverly rationed)
So not even one ~ single speck remains
High o'er (a nightingale) ~ sweet music reigns

My melodies would range ~ from low to high
Like the ocean's tide ~ and its salty smells
Beach sands offering ~ a varied supply
Of smooth pebbles and ~ empty spiral shells
Wherein their hollows ~ a sunken sea knells

  Resonating songs ~ with lengthy sustains
  Chorused by using ~ adoring refrains

Benjamin Vaccaro

Paralleling Earth ~ charting midnight skies
Our winding traces ~ commit shape to sand
Like pictures and verse ~ meant for certain eyes
And sensual themes ~ previously scanned
In nameless chapters ~ of fate's book, unplanned

Wherein it describes ~ bartering forces
Of lips and fingers ~ on a common quest
Siphoning districts ~ of all resources
Appraising landscapes ~ from valley to crest
And sequestered zones ~ with limitless zest

She woke sleeping skies ~ repeating my name
Contiguous seas ~ overheard selfsame

As frail-fallen snow ~ assumes any dint
So healers stamp care ~ in the ailing's hand
Or starry-eyed night ~ reads a telling print
Of unwritten love ~ written of in sand
Under thin-veiled sheets ~ uncovered we stand

'Neath a heel-dug shore, ~ ocean's sand compacts
As currents wash land ~ out from 'neath our toes
Four feet marooned on ~ four islanded tracts
From sequential waves' ~ unintended blows
In residual ground ~ I twigged this prose:

From shorelines of Earth ~ to Venus I aim
An offer for her ~ to carry my name

Shoulder-kissed shoulders ~ and braided fingers
Roaming oceanfront ~ encountering stars
Amid migrant dots ~ a monarch lingers
And sees us thru ~ the crimson lens of Mars
Brushing each other ~ of sand-freckled scars

Her silky palms lend ~ a passionate touch
My genuine whisks ~ from her soft face strays
Her tender strokes do ~ at least twice as much
My palms roam lower ~ and thrice surveys
Over hill and dale ~ and bi-folded maze

But inbound water ~ fills my hand-twigged claims
I redraft my bid ~ so to bond two names

Continuous tides ~ pay praise to the Moon
As fading luster ~ tucks darkness to sleep
To skin-deep waters ~ (as love is immune)
Confirming *beauty* ~ is ocean deep
And as we shall sow ~ so shall we reap

Delivering stars ~ our shoreline pledge
Chasing end of night ~ to the obverse side
Morning light dilutes ~ night's vanishing wedge
Enlightening all ~ *darkness* classified
With added clues from ~ omniscient tide

Tho' the rising Sun ~ joins our love-sick game
Cryptic stars possess ~ alternative aim

The coastline welcomes ~ the redrafted phrase
Retreating waters ~ curtsy to my dares
A defiant breeze ~ humbles warming rays
And freshens the smile ~ her honeyed face wears
Like a solar wind ~ cooling solar flares

Morning Sun ascends ~ from water to sky
To animate morn ~ and hail billing doves
At ocean's margin, ~ where wet welcomes dry
Dawn's watchful eye winks ~ at two willing loves
As only narrative ~ poets dream of

  Inquisitive skies ~ ask, "What of these claims
  Journaled twice in sand ~ that (the ocean) frames?"

Of dark and light's ~ recurring collision
Where the solar grip ~ shakes the lunar hand
Revolving tides and orbs ~ (set or risen)
Prearranged a bond ~ where bubbles swamp sand
Just destiny's eyes ~ closely understand

In sandy sheets (draped) ~ there loving grains cling
And crusts our skin ~ so shall it feeleth coarse
Daybreak's shy-red bulb ~ (reservedly brings)
Casting affection ~ (the heavens endorse)
On last evening's love ~ by a cosmic source

  Morn's infrared lamp ~ duly ordained
  Love, to those rostered ~ (who go on unnamed)

A rough sea channels ~ playful fish toward shore
(Pitching their tailfins ~ against inbound waves)
As an angler casts ~ he reels for more
While the ocean surfer ~ (a sea-swell) craves
And dismounts beside ~ memos we engraved

Persistent onslaught ~ of a sea-churned froth
Effervescing foam ~ like a witch's brew
Oceanic bonds ~ formed near briny broth
Where all-knowing waves ~ eternally knew
'Neath the harmony ~ of the love-tern's coo

Imbibing daybreak's ~ nautical champagnes
While fluttering ernes ~ bubble o'er our names

We'll rendezvous where ~ no serpent hisses
On verdant acres ~ perhaps lie a-prone
Then celebrate spring ~ with bartered kisses
And just to flowers ~ make a presence known
In blossomed fields where ~ beauty's seeds are sown

A scented wind learns ~ of lovers, downrange
And finds them vying ~ for a best embrace
Bordering heather ~ witness the exchange
But mannered roses ~ hide their blush-red face
Our grass-green history ~ zephyrs erase

Neither breeze nor gale ~ blusters the flame
To doubtful appellants ~ bring counterclaim

'Tis but a month before ~ we are to wed
Whereat shoreline sands ~ created a bond
In sanctified grains ~ (I scripted, she read)
"I love you double," ~ to which she'd respond
"As I, thrice of you, ~ furthermore beyond!"

'Twixt the gritty coast ~ and the speckled sky
She and I frequent ~ there to lie between
From deep outer space ~ to love's inner thigh
Only star and grain ~ discern all we mean
'Neath heaven's glisten ~ (whereon sands we lean)

Eternal love ~ ever crops sugar cane
And death parts no one ~ so to meet again

Then the ocean rinsed ~ my promise away
Laundered my scribble ~ at heaven's behest
And apathy's stars ~ loomed in disarray
Breaching alignments ~ (earlier professed)
To granular coasts ~ whereon lovebirds nest

Why did (my memo) ~ seawater dissolve
Drowned by shifting ~ and unpublished tides
I defy such a sign ~ to (us) involve
Does predestined fate, ~ in each star reside
And did they, in me, ~ an omen, confide?

Twinkling dialects ~ sadly declaim
"'Tis underwater ~ that overcame"

One dreamy evening ~ while we were sailing
Restless waves summoned ~ an ill-equipped stern
Surprise's element ~ vetoed bailing
The vessel listed ~ from the ocean's churn
To our love-marked shore ~ she could not return

From time to time ~ I come to kneel and etch
A loving memo ~ in the beachfront sands
Perpetual tides ~ never cease to fetch
And export touch ~ from terrestrial hands
To an unchained soul ~ sunk in unmapped lands

On the sandy coast ~ where *love*, fate named
Alas, I sketched: *Why ~ you, the deep-sea claimed?*

Finis

* *Binary stars* - a two-star system that revolves about their common center of mass - and yes, they're separated by *heaven* (or euphemistically, *ecstasy*)

Castle rooms, and other areas (if ya' know what I mean)

- ➤ **Bailey** - a courtyard within the walls of the castle
- ➤ **Bottlery** - for storing and dispensing wines and other expensive provisions, typically located between the Great Hall and Kitchen.
- ➤ **Bower** – a private area, for the Lady of the castle, used as a withdrawing-room and bedroom.

➢ **Chapel** – available to all members of the castle household for prayer, usually close to the Great Hall, and often two stories high, with the nave divided horizontally. The Lord's family and dignitaries sat in the upper part and the servants occupied the lower part

➢ **Dungeon** - for holding prisoners and usually found in an underground room of one of the towers

➢ **Gatehouse** - a multiplex of towers, bridges, and barriers built to protect the main entrance

➢ **Great Hall** – a main area for meeting and dining, and used by everyone who lived in the castle. A large one-room structure with a loft ceiling. At the end of the Great Hall was the Dais, a raised platform for a high table where the highest ranking Lord and Nobles sat**.**

➢ **Mezzanine** - the landing between two main stories

➢ **Pantry** - for storage of perishable food products

➢ **Turrets** - a small tower rising above, and resting on, one of the main towers, usually used as a lookout

Morning's Verdict

Picture the loveliest ~ unlocking her eyes
As the morning Sun ~ from dark is risen
Both expressions flaunt ~ captivating guise
By releasing light ~ they held in prison

Arresting wavelengths ~ remanded thru night
That morning's verdict ~ acquits by sight

Finis

Polarity

Decency scowls ~ at the face of evil
Panic veils itself ~ 'neath the sham of pride
Hostile nerve appoints ~ the hostile devil
Chronic addition ~ equals multiplied
Yet everywhere has ~ not a place to hide

  Nighttime purifies ~ what daytime soils
  As Newton's third ~ inversely recoils

War ignites fire ~ in pursuit of me
Overcome by rage ~ swamped in friendless flame
But peace lends its hand ~ of serenity
And points respect's finger ~ at me in shame
Then shakes: *what better foe ~ doth water tame?*

  Abject silliness, ~ by fury, tempted
  Quelled by sanity ~ knowledge pre-empted

A psychiatrist speaks ~ on carnal lust
Perverted preachers ~ define *forbidden*
An airless ember ~ horny to combust
(Like pubescent will ~ solely id-ridden)
That super-ego ~ keeps deftly hidden

  For current temptation ~ I discarded
  What once (in my prime) ~ rashly regarded

As arrogance snarls ~ at heavenly stars
Reticence genuflects ~ to common earth
Pride's skin exhibits ~ greed's envious scars
As modesty (blind) ~ tallies neither worth
Nor sees appraisal ~ in self-serving mirth

 Instead of soaring ~ o'er the highest mound
 Meekly, I tread ~ on pedestrian ground

Free-thinking Buddhists ~ learn to die, to live
The eloquent speak ~ thru perceptive ear
They taught me: *tis worse ~ to receive than give*
Eclipsed background stars ~ are not as they appear
The caring statesman ~ in fact, insincere

 Very much differs ~ with observation
 As inner planets' ~ retro-rotation

In sixty-minutes ~ her prettiness fails
Like the glory of ~ the morning hour
But over him which ~ nothing else prevails
(Neither pine, shrub, ~ nor glorious flower)
Is the thousand-year'd, ~ tall redwood tower

 Calendar, yardstick, ~ lengthy, quick, or short
 Einsteinian clocks ~ tick time's fickle sport

The element's trait ~ in combination
Resembles nothing ~ of its former guise
And phantom presence ~ (post amputation)
Whereupon recall ~ sensation relies
And do not gamblers ~ self-burglarize?

  The light ray's path is ~ as Euclidean
  As Rome's longitude ~ prime meridian

Comedy sobs ~ at a grim finale
As tragedy cackles ~ at the joker
When laziness weeps ~ meaningless dally
Aspiration laughs ~ at mediocre
Purchased and sold ~ by ambition's broker

  Tho' *before* was ~ overcome by *after*
  A clown of sorrow ~ perished in laughter

A rainbow supplants ~ the grey cloud ashen
Whilst pity cowers ~ to meaningless spite
A moon-lit vista ~ eclipsed in fashion
But the well-dressed day, ~ sports Sun's trendy light
And innocent prey ~ (guilty fangs) indict

  The artistic hand ~ that would shadow us
  Loans subtractive tint ~ brushing minus plus

There is loss within ~ decisive winning
Felonious crime ~ in the defender
Concluding one thing ~ brings new beginning
Welcome dividends ~ in quick surrender
Of your fictions, both ~ Buyer and Vendor

  Motion's consequence ~ on receding forms
  Reddens truth way past ~ believable norms

Transitory leaves ~ shall grow and wither
Night's attentive eye ~ shall eclipse and shine
But every daybreak, ~ thither and hither
Rendezvous at ~ the horizontal line
Where again with morn ~ sunbeams recombine

  To wax and wane ~ like seasonal flowers
  Who, by consumption ~ themselves devour

Karmic cycles claim: ~ *effect precedes cause*
So *interest* asks ~ of an expedition
Whose beginning point ~ (free inquiry) draws
On: *how the traveler ~ reached start's position*
The mind's lens is ground ~ by the logician

  Does the moon fall toward ~ or draw upon earth
  And are sentients ~ recycling birth

John, chapter seven, ~ beckons *chance* for peace
Imagines above us ~ only hell-less skies
Nudity campaigning ~ warfare surcease
But his clothes of love ~ fit everyone's size
Illogically slain ~ 'neath Dakota's eyes

  A verse from Paul ~ believes in yesterday
  Tomorrow never knows ~ it was today

There are accounts ~ in recent articles
Whereby *destruction* ~ befriends *creation*
They cited anti- ~ matter particle's
Displacement of ~ quantum perturbation
As now's date possessed ~ no expiration

  Relativity, ~ while drafted in Bern
  Sub-atomic thugs ~ murder time at CERN

There was a mystic ~ named Polarity
Wherein *nothingness,* ~ with *all* collided
When divergence met ~ singularity
Or infinite thought ~ alone resided
It preached, "One is two ~ just twice divided"

  She cautions ~ *who hesitates, lost is he*
  Look, then again, ~ before we leap, must we

Impoverished world ~ and of all you boast
Youth and promise ~ being momentary
And carnal conquest ~ (which you value most)
Or dream affluence ~ as necessary
And modesty as ~ an adversary

Before I'd thrive ~ on deceit's pretension
Blandly, I'll mature ~ on honor's pension

Finis

Reigning Skies

Zeppelins commanding ~ over northwest skies.
Like dismal war-craft ~ (for targets) trollin'
Airborne equipment ~ mutely advertise
Menacing silence ~ like thunder rollin'
With threatening looks, ~ grim, gray, and swollen

  Gloomy stares from ~ the poker-faced city
  Hushed voices of ~ a sunless committee

Like rowdy masses ~ above competing
Or a band of thugs ~ in mob-like cluster
With no indication ~ of retreating
Day's vote for sunlight ~ they filibuster
In battleship gray ~ devoid of luster

  Errant hooligans ~ in violent gangs
  On shady corners, ~ darkness overhangs

Their leader incites ~ partisan babble
From a lofty post ~ 'gins to sermonize
Then old grey bigots ~ arousing rabble
Preaching *unity* ~ lectured *polarize*
In dialogue (charged) ~ highly ionized

  "To infectious rays" ~ they vaccinated
  "We're immunized ~ un-illuminated"

Robbing sequoias ~ of soaring shadows
Rendering lilies ~ morose and cheerless
Pilfering glisten ~ from grassy meadows
Whose lush green smiles ~ typify *peerless*
Saddens the joyful ~ formerly tearless

Their inbound journey ~ strikes brilliance duller
Crowning the rainbow ~ with more discolor

Sentencing dawn ~ to a term in prison
As morning's glimmer ~ is under indict
The penitentiary ~ daybreak is in
Like an outdoor jail ~ underneath their flight
As honest day melts ~ in counterfeit night

Sunlight for sundials ~ ungainly shapes thieve
Condemning daytime ~ to synthetic eve

An orchestra high ~ above assembling
Detuned to the key ~ of symphonic grey
As the wind section ~ began trembling
Percussive darkness ~ drummed high-noon away
A nocturne on light- ~ diminishing day

Sharpened harmonics ~ in orchestration
Jointly banding ~ for precipitation

The key of dreary ~ starts the overture
As tearful dewdrops ~ in adagio
But counter rhythms ~ in time's signature
Pluck pizzicato ~ gales, arpeggio
And to thunder's god ~ an omaggio

Dissonance of ~ charged electrostatics
Burst in the key ~ of *mono-chromatics*

Lightning wands chairing ~ the whirlwind sections
Double-reed heatwaves ~ as weathermen cast
Fight cacophonous ~ cold-front convections
As poor-tensioned strings ~ with bassoons contrast
Insecurely tuned ~ by a leader, half-assed

Or a podiumed ~ un-taut instructor
More cleverly still ~ *semi-conductor*

Dirigibles of ~ dark hostility
Wet raining bullets ~ 'neath reigning masses
Tho' no predictions ~ of tranquility
Peace triumphs over ~ grey warring gases
Unexpectedly ~ the onslaught passes

From atmospheric ~ governing bullies
To cumulus peace- ~ brokering woolies

Criminal charges ~ from the troposphere
On regions to be ~ electrocuted
For passing time served ~ prosecutions clear
Lightning penalties ~ unexecuted
Shocking offenses ~ nature commuted

Dropping charges to ~ which clouds enslaved
Unjust sentences ~ Mother Nature waived

I remember a sky ~ wherein they gathered
Warned on radio's ~ sports, weather, and news
Defenseless puddles ~ beat 'til they lathered
Formed little tide pools ~ and boulevard brews
The *Welcome* door mat ~ scours mud from shoes

At a post-noon auction ~ the beaming Sun sells
Vending warmth to birds, ~ light, voltaic cells

Finis

Romantic Andalusia

The lush olive trees ~ of Andalusia
Are warmly fanned ~ by oceanic wind
Two echoed smiles ~ in crimson fuchsia
Adorns a niña[1] ~ delightfully grinned
And duplicate sis ~ attractively twinned

  Some quarry iron ~ in distant mountains
  Others toss copper ~ in luck-filled fountains

Moorish appointments ~ flavor southwest Spain
Kaolinic[2] hills ~ sing *terracotta*
A fleeting drizzle ~ mists a field of grain
As guitarists croon ~ Lara's *Granada*
A glazier taps shape ~ to stained glass solder

  Tiled verandas ~ host clannish flowers
  Sipping fresh distilled ~ Spanish showers

On cobblestone streets ~ of west Chiclana
Sidewalk gypsies vend ~ laced flamenco arms
As love courses thru ~ the Guadiana[3]
It kisses the loam ~ of bordering farms
Riverside growers ~ trade organic charms

  In a hallowed dell ~ enclosed in birches
  A vicarage prays ~ 'tween two stone churches

A painter strokes ~ a Sevillian landscape
As dreamy yachts ~ populate her harbor
A blinded sculptress ~ carves a wooden shape
While black moustaches ~ trim graying barbers
Young lovers kissing ~ 'neath shady arbors

Eye-catching hombres ~ in broad sombreros
Bidding girls to dance ~ Ravel's *Boléro*

Eucalyptus scents ~ a Málagan breeze
A museum nearby ~ tells Cubism's[4] tale
Delis promoting ~ local picón cheese
Whetting appetite ~ with every inhale
Aromatics passed ~ by a clement gale

Ancient waves blemish ~ her Atlantic shore
Telling vintage tales ~ about tides of war

Finis

1.   Niña – Spanish for *girl*
2.   Kaolin is clay
3.   Guadiana – a river in Andalusia
4.   *Cubism* was a 20th century avant-garde art movement. Pablo Picasso (and
     Georges Braque) are said to have fathered this artistic style.

The Ageless Aquarian

Quantum Narratives

From the distant star ~ in outermost space
To Earth's prettiest ~ with the charming grin
Neither overthrow ~ time's eternal pace
But for the heavenly ~ premise herein
Nor relativity's ~ paradox-ed twin[1]

  On lengthy ages ~ sweet wines relieth
  Her unfading watch ~ still time defieth

To mythical gods ~ a sweet Cup-bearer
Like the youthful glow ~ burned in Hebe's eyes
Or dilation's clock[2] ~ whose face grows fairer
And hands run counter ~ to normal clock-wise
A constellation ~ in October's skies

  Retro-handedness ~ seemingly ironic
  Eons patented ~ eternity's tonic

Like Eos, she could be ~ Orion's lover
Or a timeless sketch ~ in an artist's tome
On an author's first ~ maybe grace the cover
Or radiant theme ~ offered in a poem
With all theatrics ~ of a monochrome

  Two dreams divided ~ by twelve thousand days
  Amidst blackened strands ~ neither whites nor greys

A hand of kindness ~ and heart of honey
Laughter in debt ~ to intelligent wit
A face to silkscreen ~ on royal money
And bedchamber eyes ~ dreaming-ly twi-lit
That Intaglio's press ~ could not counterfeit

  When undertaking ~ to etch an image
  I'd forge to coinage ~ her timeless visage

I'd strike the portrait ~ on shillings and dimes
Assign the smile ~ to a lucky charm
To offset the jinxed ~ 'gainst frost-bitten times
And warm the luckless ~ thru fate's icy harm
Bringing peace to Jews ~ har-mo-ny Islam

  Permanence cherished ~ as Egyptian gold
  Immunizing youth ~ from increasing old

When I cast textures ~ and shades of her face
And monetize aspects ~ crimson tinted
Or emboss thereon ~ her eternal grace
Luxuriant silk ~ graciously printed
Then freely hand out ~ currency minted

  Redeeming to all ~ bearers on demand
  Ever's hourglass ~ dripping ageless sand

Finis

1. **Twin Paradox:**

   o   In Einstein's theory of Special Relativity, the concept of Twin Paradox involves identical twins. One, of the pair, makes a high-velocity journey into space and returns home to discover the twin, on Earth, aged more. Essentially, time "slowed down" proportional to the velocity acting upon the travelling body.

   In theory, if one travels beyond the speed of light, they biologically age backwards, but this postulate has numerous complexities.

2. **Time dilation**:

   o   Example 1: Imagine a pair of identical clocks; one in an attic and the other, a basement. They run at different rates because they have different gravitational influences acting upon them. The *time dilation* is the difference between the two clocks.

   o   Example 2: Imagine a pair of identical clocks; one at rest and the other in motion. They run at different rates because they have different forces of motion acting upon them. The *time dilation* is the difference between the two clocks.

The Autopsy of Odette

At Braydon's pastel ~ sadly gazed Odette
Purring melodies ~ he'd frequently sing
But destiny's clock ~ untimely reset
The unwed hand ~ with an engagement ring

Uncapping one ~ of his darling colognes
Sniffing remembrance ~ with every inhale
Unhappiness from ~ melancholic groans
Stifles the merry, ~ mutes the Nightingale

Thru the swirl of leaves ~ by a restless squall
And crunching footsteps ~ specific to fall
With Braydon's likeness ~ makes a routine call

Behind rusted gates ~ at Cider Mill Lane
A pasture yields ~ to monumental stone
There Braydon rests ~ in a lifeless domain
A fathom below ~ all that's overgrown

Odette weeps a tale ~ of briny showers
'Neath the canopy ~ of an ancient pine
Spattered droplets ~ irrigate flowers
Purchased to garden ~ Bray's un-gardened shrine

Staring at the art ~ grieving o'er his tomb
With a heart stabbed ~ by unspeakable gloom
Romeo's Juliet ~ meets premature doom

Twilight deserts her ~ lying in the field
As a midnight rain ~ spatters muddy beads
On her lifeless face ~ spots of dirt congealed
And neglected blades ~ of adjacent weeds

Morning remembers ~ two earthly lovers
Of open beauty ~ with love unburied
The departed pair ~ sodden earth covers
Odette, above ground, ~ both cemeteried

For causative paths ~ of Odette's demise
Clinicians presumed, ~ medics theorized:
Into sudden death ~ *woe* metastasized

A specialist gives ~ an initial check
Notes cheeks overdosed ~ on salinity
Brackish streams hemorrhaged ~ striating her neck
While *grief's* numbers crossed ~ *risk's* vicinity

Not any of which ~ acutely sicken
'Twas something perhaps ~ heard, inhaled, or viewed
But would dissection ~ pinpoint *woe-stricken*
Bidding other grounds ~ with more certitude

Finding no blockage ~ her airways unbound
The Desk Reference hints: ~ *Perhaps in sorrow drowned*
Under *Causation* ~ the autopsy found:

It spots *reminiscence* ~ swelling her brain
Observes *commitment* ~ choking one finger
Tho' love coursed freely ~ it hindered each vein
Hinting death came swift ~ and did not linger

And to the retinas ~ Bray's likeness fused
Ruled *doubtful* as cause, ~ pathologists say
But pressing 'Dette's ribs ~ one final breath oozed
Matching aroma ~ whiffed the prior day

A nurse bids account ~ for parts unspoken
As unchecked regions ~ give specific token
Something else may be ~ fatally broken

The zest of her lips, ~ dripped sweet aftertaste
Her thorax ravaged ~ by embracement's wound
Injured legs proved much ~ to his grave, she raced
Her ears echoed vows ~ and ditties Bray crooned

Alas, an organ ~ found over-beaten
Massively attacked ~ by lost affection
And like bees' honey ~ 'twas over-sweetened
Scrubbing any need ~ for more dissection

The coroner drafts ~ the decedent's chart
Noting Odette's hands ~ still clutching the art
And Braydon's image ~ consuming her heart

Finis

Quantum Narratives

The Eyes Inside My Lids

Nightly 'neath ~ my lidded region
  two eyes from ~ a far-flung legion
  and for some ~ symbolic reason
  permeate ~ my two flesh shades

Whilst I sense ~ with visage streaming
  am I awake ~ or just dreaming
  of an essence ~ onetime gleaming
  beaming likeness ~ here portrayed

"Have me you bid?" ~ in sleep, I asked
  scheming pupils ~ play charade

Nothing answered, ~ nothing said

Softly asking ~ (as I'm lying)
  are my eyes ~ with doom allying
  or are watchful ~ eyes implying:
  we have flown ~ with you before

Below my lids ~ quite austerely
  misty visions ~ waxing clearly
  in a district ~ lying nearly
  merely 'neath ~ the optic fore

"Who is that?" ~ I do inquire
  "dearly you?" ~ I do outpour

No reaction ~ as before

Each night to sleep, ~ when I adjourn
  'neath my two lids, ~ two themes return
  like darkness in ~ a Field[1] nocturne
  which the soundest ~ sense forbade

Thru idyllic ~ dark dimension
  photons falling ~ from suspension
  beacons planning ~ intervention
  but how is it ~ they pervade

Two beams from ~ another kingdom
  mention facts ~ from whence they strayed

Trying softly ~ to persuade

During slumber ~ (when descended)
  steeped in dreaming ~ arms extended
  itinerants ~ to me, wended
  masked as faceless ~ eyes I saw

'Tween lid-locked eyes ~ and midnight's air
  and sallow, wispy, ~ filmy hair
  translucent eyes ~ back at me stare
  like a yachtsman ~ casing shore

Avoiding shallows ~ that might snare
  for deeper gist ~ oarsmen yaw

Like I, as eyes ~ lingered o'er

As if happy ~ with more sorrow
 from those pupils ~ *woe* I'd borrow
 which by sunrise ~ of the morrow
 left me guessing ~ the charade

Daybreak witnessed ~ my eyes blinking
 as noon studied ~ my mind thinking
 that eve prior, ~ was I drinking
 absinthe or ~ a hardened ade

Causing wonders ~ like mirages
 with the real world ~ disarrayed

Laws of physics ~ un-obeyed

Nameless gazes ~ surely taking
 pleasure that my ~ joints were aching
 and that my ~ chilled bones were quaking
 shaking from a ~ shine of yore

Were these two beams, ~ at me, laughing
 or effects of ~ excess quaffing
 while they stared, ~ they eyed me chaffing
 graphing regions ~ to explore

'Tween lid and lens ~ and precincts near
 drafting sectors ~ that they saw

All these districts ~ maybe more

In rapt cadence ~ pupils walking
  metered verses ~ of eyes talking
  sheerly clearly ~ they were stalking
  gawking thru ~ their covert raid

Trundling eyes ~ in double file
  traipsing halls ~ of bloodless smiles
  as I rested ~ all the while
  valid pallid ~ pupils paid

Visits to my ~ domicile
  in wavelengths in ~ untitled shade

Neither brown ~ nor bluish grayed

Inverse lenses ~ bent on masking
  bizarre questions ~ they are asking
  'neath my lids ~ in darkness basking
  seeking 'sylum ~ whilst I snore

But these peering ~ eyes so candid
  beckon (me) whilst ~ they demanded
  like a phantom ~ who commanded
  silhouettes ~ to hover o'er

Out of time ~ but inside reason
  stranded between ~ either/or

Here and there yet, ~ neither/nor

And when resting ~ *wish* would glimmer
 yet when awake ~ *hope* grew dimmer
 below my lids, ~ figures shimmer
 frequencies ~ that ricocheted

Nameless sightings ~ of my making
 could be conjures ~ of un-waking
 was my brain ~ (both eyes) forsaking
 faking dreams ~ therein displayed

Forgeries ~ of wanton guile
 breaking contracts ~ sense obeyed

The optic nerve ~ of unfair trade

Retinas free from ~ vein occlusions
 yet saw only ~ blurred illusions
 and impinging ~ strange intrusions
 radiating ~ *yester-yore*

Are there inner ~ wizards jeering
 toying with my ~ sense of hearing
 I am seeing ~ shining nearing
 veering me ~ toward furthermore

By diffraction ~ thru time's prism
 peering from ~ a stellar shore

Guiding flickers ~ semaphore

My palsied tongue ~ (tied from screaming)
 panic silenced ~ during dreaming
 etheric beams ~ keep on beaming
 from a ghostly ~ soul a-strayed

Why would such a ~ vision nightly
 visit me ~ as I slept tightly
 yet obscure ~ itself politely
 lightly like a ~ serenade

Or a nocturne ~ keyed in minor
 nightly while ~ two eyes that played

Drum rolls 'neath ~ my lid's parade

For this puzzle, ~ I was piecing
 two reflections ~ most unceasing
 a link perhaps ~ is increasing
 to a lassie ~ ages fore

Tell me if my ~ eyes are failing
 why apneic ~ (yet inhaling)
 why, my hunch, ~ hers try derailing
 veiling meaning ~ heretofore

Tell me seer ~ of this presence
 tailing eyes ~ I can't ignore

Why eyelids (two) ~ are housing four

To whom do these ~ lone eyes belong
  and (for a host) ~ appear to long
  my unease, I ~ cannot prolong
  please conclude ~ this escapade

Such a sub-lid ~ ceaseless taunting
  finding sport ~ in sport-less haunting
  theorizing ~ those eyes (flaunting)
  dwell in one ~ departed maid

Lovelorn Wilis ~ unrequited
  Giselle redeems ~ love unpaid

Dancing death ~ in forest's shade

Theaters dimmed ~ host lightless faces
  detached eyes ~ inhabit spaces
  witnesses ~ from astral places
  testify to ~ scenes of yore

Have my eyes ~ begun allying
  with strange vistas ~ cast for dying
  and does it not ~ merit trying
  tying gist ~ to scenes they saw

And that those eyes ~ thrice lived in one
  more lustrous than ~ lost Lenore

Tho' she journeyed ~ aft and fore

Quantum Narratives

Headlining in ~ dramatic games
  an absent actress ~ (title) claims
  to two moving ~ filmic frames
  whereon my panels ~ previews played

As the theater ~ screen kept showing
  scenes from Dead-gar ~ Allan Poe-ing
  nevermore and ~ ever-flowing
  Lenorean ~ eyes she rayed

Radiant, rare, ~ and once glowing
  blackbird crowing ~ only said

One shriek from ~ his stock in trade

'Neath sunless lids ~ phantasms shined
  wherein four virtues ~ recombined
  and frequencies ~ (of altered kind)
  guide me toward ~ her optic shore

Sleeping eyes ~ in nightly session
  and when closed ~ invoke regression
  to a once ~ well-known expression
  that was here ~ and then no more

Swallowed by ~ another kingdom
  carnal eyesight ~ never saw

From me, distanced ~ as I snore

                                      Benjamin Vaccaro

Optic trysts ~ with discarnation
 As four eyes share ~ in flirtation
 telepathic ~ consummation
 'cross a mortal ~ barricade

This convex-concave ~ eye affair
 in private meet ~ such that both pair
 stay unsighted ~ yet at each glare
 where fond pupils ~ masquerade

As likenesses, ~ to each, aware
 'til the comely ~ visions fade

To a hue ~ in ghostly jade

Distant shine ~ for growing reason
 of greenish eyes ~ once in season
 guiltless of ~ ocular treason
 on liners where ~ both gleams I saw

Travelers ~ without conditions
 voyaging ~ as apparitions
 emanating ~ light transmissions
 audition nightly ~ for the chore

Of plucking midnight's ~ melody
 commissioned eyes ~ strum a score

More tuneful than ~ raven's caw

Like the dead ~ (in allegory)
 who extolled ~ hereafter's story
 return to laud ~ all its glory
 blinded souls ~ to heaven prayed

In need of ~ divine optician
 to redeem ~ their eyes' condition
 and to channel ~ sweet musicians
 to (other senses) ~ serenade

Flanked by singing ~ winging angels
 dark renditions ~ she replayed

As dirges in ~ my eyed parade

But hearing in ~ the Bardo state
 in after-death ~ helps liberate
 and *impermanence* ~ reinstate
 realms past (says ~ Tibetan lore)

Numb to earthly ~ tribulations
 memories ~ of mad frustrations
 undone carnal ~ stimulations
 shedding egos ~ once I wore

And waken to ~ former knowledge
 of vibrations ~ long before

With two eyes ~ that oversaw

                   Benjamin Vaccaro

My optic nerve ~ notwithstanding
 myopic views, ~ un-expanding
 what are your ~ lone eyes demanding
 why do they ~ seek to invade

The eyes inside ~ my lids are trying
 to see why eyes ~ keep applying
 for tenancy ~ (occupying)
 prying thru ~ a barricade

Or just perchance ~ on assignment
 to escort me ~ unafraid

As a cosmic ~ travel aide

Inquiry's lens ~ confirmed benign
 when once with hers ~ would intertwine
 mirroring one ~ another's shine
 as *absolutely* ~ is to *sure*

By daybreak of ~ a newer dawn
 Gabriel[2] wafts ~ a golden horn
 trumpeting realms ~ forever born
 in wavelengths from ~ an ancient shore

And primeval ~ thought is drawn
 visioning visions ~ dreamt before

Of the kingdom ~ *Evermore*

Quantum Narratives

Incognito ~ nightly gaming
 fondly during ~ dreaming aiming
 lenses at me ~ keep proclaiming
 naming purpose ~ why they strayed

Now I'm seeing ~ all the seeing
 are thru eyes ~ loaned from a being
 to a spirit ~ for its fleeing
 freeing self ~ from Earth's charade

Palliating ~ infant blindness
 seeing darkness ~ not as shade

But mortal fears ~ go on as they'd

Two eyes 'neath ~ my fleshy cover
 as I observed, ~ they'd just hover
 likely fit ~ an earthly lover
 from a timeless ~ time before

For no longer ~ meaning, mining
 why eyes hike ~ across my lining
 during night- ~ by-night's reclining
 finding byways ~ for the tour

Clearing customs ~ for a passage
 Priming trails ~ for nevermore

By the lifeless ~ lass of yore

To astral planes ~ (a soul) promoting
 reversed eyes ~ above me floating
 released from a ~ tissue coating
 watching human ~ housing fade

From somatic ~ transmutation
 to etheric ~ incarnation
 taking earthly ~ adoration
 to the soul ~ who nightly bade

To disengage ~ my silver cord
 for destinations ~ lastly made

With a lifeless ~ living maid

Finis

1. John Field (Sept. 1782 - 1837) an Irish pianist, composer, and teacher, known as the inventor of the nocturne

2. In mathematics, Gabriel's horn is also known as Torricelli's Trumpet. It's a geometric irony, where the shape has finite volume but infinite surface area. Gabriel, was an Archangel who blows the horn to announce Judgment Day. Here I take poetic license to loosely imply a connection between the infinitude of afterlife (or pre-life) and the finiteness of conscious, bodily life.

Yule

'Tis the time of year ~ when the snowman thrives
And woodsmen gather ~ oaken logs to split
Worker bees nestle ~ in temperate hives
As fresh-fallen leaves ~ to the ground commit
We shake out sweaters ~ mother's, mother knit

  At the edge of sky ~ (where Sun suspends)
  Ere the gray day 'gins ~ it, no sooner, ends

A flock of blackbirds ~ peppers drifts of snow
Tapered 'cicles fringe ~ overhanging eaves
A mother fawneth ~ o'er her untrained doe
Like infants nestled ~ in parental sleeves
A snowman's pipe, ~ snatched by boyish thieves

  As clever owls preen ~ 'neath layered feathers
  Clouds negotiate ~ blustery weathers

Glacial fog provokes ~ our dwindling breath
Tyrannical wind ~ frightens leaves from trees
Thirsty grass staring ~ in the face of death
'Til spring sun tempers ~ winter's hostile freeze
Would not clement rain ~ (all the Earth) appease?

  Outside my window ~ two pose-a-silling
  A dove-ly couple, ~ rehearse-a-billing

While pestling scented ~ mulling spices
Clara relocates ~ a nosy spider
Glowing cinders chase ~ rude winter's ices
As she decants fresh- ~ pressed steaming cider
Apple-cheeked fry ~ ride a snowy glider

 A pungent kitchen ~ of nutmeg'd fragrance
 Tchaikovsky's soldiers ~ waltz snow-flaked cadence

As a purring hearth ~ flaunts glowing embers
Brimming soup glances ~ o'er a black-cast pot
Destitute puppets ~ from past Decembers
Unselfish hands ~ (to the orphaned) allot
Dawn's fragrant tale ~ expressed the coffee pot

 A winding fence of ~ endless posts and beams
 Fades to horizon's ~ ice-crowned evergreens

Cheer winter's banquet, ~ hoist a ruby glass
Recognition bid, ~ for lasting good fate
A prim wax candle ~ over tarnished brass
Wanes and curtsies on ~ all-too-soon a date
Goodnight and sweetness ~ to my honeyed mate

 To the sylph, the gnome, ~ the Pagan, and fool
 We toast the season ~ on this feast of Yule

Finis

Synopsis

Some chit-chat about a few of the selections in this book.

A Romantic Poet - I am a bit of a dreamer

Decimation of the English - One needs only to look at spelling in the days of Chaucer, grammar in the days of Shakespeare, and numerical substitutes for words in the twenty-first century, to realize language is alive. I'm guessing it's generational, and the older typically judge the younger.

Indecent Exposure - The title was supposed to draw attention because it's a topic worthy of it. 5G radiation is masquerading as a *convenience technology*, in wireless devices, and towers are going up everywhere. It can damage DNA in anything living (this means DNA in a woman's eggs and the mitochondrial DNA in the eggs of an unborn female fetus, and the next female, and the next – FOREVER!). This progression may irreversibly alter the human species. There is a rising body of evidence about the broad-spectrum dangers of EMF (electro-magnetic frequencies). Some data has been around for decades, but sequestered from the public. Many respectable authorities, agencies, and peer-reviewed studies, await your curiosity. I hint to a few sources in the rhyming invective presented here. Additionally, I tossed in a few condemnations about pharmaceuticals, food toxins, vaccines, and other government/corporate insanities. Like many products, the industrialists don't have to prove their goods are safe, you have to prove they aren't. And until you do, availability remains!

Joey and Her Jax - Based on a true story about the death of my daughter's pet. Of course, here and there, I toss in a few surrealistic imageries, but the basic premise is real. The first draft of this was during my daughter's term at law school. Now and then, I helped her with an essay, and seemingly, a few terms colonized my brain and found their way into this poem, and others.

Memo in the Sand - For the majority of my life, I lived on the south shore Long Island, NY, one mile from an ocean. And yes, back in the day, many fond evenings were spent there. Moonlight, wind, impatient waters, solitude, sand, stars, no beeping gadgetry, and a dose of youth. Given these components, it's easy to compose a fantasy.

Polarity - Having exposure to ironies in science, seeing the oxymora in life, and the paradoxes couched in world philosophies and religions, one easily knits a rhyming commentary with a few of these "polarizing" notions.

The Autopsy of Odette – A scientific title involving a romantic ailment – death from a broken heart. I like to merge dimensions, even if slightly implausible. For instance: *Reminiscence* isn't known to "swell" one's brain, any more than *commitment* chokes a finger; but the ideas are close enough to just keep it from wandering into the absurd, because *reminiscence* is in the brain and an engagement (or commitment) encircles the ring finger, so the perceptions are in reach.

The Eyes Inside My Lids - Based on a pair of eyes that visited me, in a recurring, somewhat poignant, dream. The "visitors" existed between the outer layer of my eyes and the inner "liner" of my eyelids, hence, *The Eyes inside My Lids*. When my eyes opened, nothing was there. The eyes remain unidentified.

This piece is the only departure from pentameter, and an opportunity to exploit alliteration. It follows the internal rhyming, and syllabic pacing of Edgar Allen Poe's, *The Raven* (quarter tempo for you musicians, with a "rest" whenever there's 7 syllables). I even "borrowed" a bit of the master's imagery and rationale. For instance: because of its close union to beauty, Poe (and numerous writers) chose death, often of a young woman, as an expressive mechanism to convey the certainty that awaits us. Here I deed "title" of the eyes, to one departed human, from ago, and whose soul is cyclic, and laced it into a metaphysical tale, about the death of a beautiful being, more "rare and radiant" than lost Lenore.

Acknowledgements & Credits

A nod to those offering open-minded appraisal of my work, and other inspirations:

Donna Adams, Gene Adams, Dominick Amatulli, Shona Anderson, Stephen Bezas, Joseph Crosson, Valerie Crosson, Jordana Desernia, Thomas Desernia, Eileen Feinman, John Fenimore, McKenna Fenimore, Nancy Fenimore, Cheryl Frank, Amy Bates-Garone, Tony Garone, Brad Greenspan, Barry Hauser, Anne Leighton, Dennis McDermott, Debby Michaels, JJ Michaels, Joey Michaels, Rosanna Mitchell, Dave Neer, †Toba Neer, JoAnne Politano, Bruna Scalisi, Joe Scalisi, Leonardo Scalisi, Beverly Seaver, Erica Sloane, Sean Strommer, Charlie Vaccaro, †Mae Vaccaro

Poets Performance Association: Cliff Bleidner (Co-founder) Lorraine Conlin (Nassau County Poet Laureate Emeritus) James Romano (Executive member, awarded poet, charter member of the Norman Mailer Society)

†Antonia Van Loon (née Smith) - An author, tutor, Mensan, and cousin from the days of yore

Photo	Page	Identity	Photographer
Front Cover		Debra	Debra Bonomo Michaels
Dedication Page	5	Mom, Dad, and Brother	Who knows?
Joey and Her Jax	37	Joey	Debra Bonomo Michaels
Joey and Her Jax	37	†Jax	Joey Michaels Andreaccio
The Ageless Aquarian	97	Debra	Debra Bonomo Michaels
A Great Pet	125	†Snorkel	Benjamin Vaccaro
Rear Cover		Benjamin Vaccaro	Joey Michaels Andreaccio

A Bit about Me and Where I Harvest Thoughts and Words

To name a few things, I:

Venerate the Sun * Love Debby * Play guitar and know a bit of music theory * Came out of this world, not into it * Keep/kept an organic garden * Love dogs * Fear the topics corporate media omits * Am wild about the first and second movements of Beethoven's 9th Symphony * Dabbled in Real Estate and  Homebuilding * Juice * Fear Monsanto * Think Ralph Nader matters * Wear mostly black clothing * Work/worked as a CNC programmer and draftsman * Know the difference between education and knowledge * Am appalled by the misuse of modern technology * Am a vegetarian (nearly 30-years) * Think the James Ossuary has a story to tell the world * Distill my own water * Would like a 1959 Fender Bassman® * Am an expert at nothing * Know we're in the universe, and the universe is in us * Majored in Theoretical Physics at Adelphi University * Grew up on a diet of astute proverbs offered by my mother * Am flawed (but that's its own book) * Believe all food should be organic * Learned a little Martial arts * Am captivated by the precision in ancient measuring systems and sacred geometry * Wish I could tutor the unlettered * Still appreciate tokens of influence, by certain family members, no longer casting shadows; they were Mensans * Believe medicine is your food and food your medicine (within reason) * Co-owned a gymnastics and ballet school * Like rogue Egyptologists * Fear mandated vaccines * Think a half-truth is a whole lie * Challenge the rationale for pathologizing normal juvenile behavior, then medicating children accordingly * Believe the Sphinx was built before the last ice-age ended * Owned a small architectural woodworking company * Do Rubick's Cube and Rubick's Revenge (they keep the brain supple) * Studied classical ballet from André Eglevsky and other Russian greats (this was about 40-pounds ago) * Relish: *the Raven, Venus and Adonis, the Rubaiyat,* and *the Rape of Lucrece* * Am diminished by another's hunger (pity the hungry, but more, pity those who won't feed them) * Spend far too much time explaining negatives cannot be proven (ya' know: *absence of proof is not proof of absence*) * Could re-write *Gone with the Wind,* referencing a world no longer * Love fresh bread and exotic cuisine * Know the only thing constant, is change * Know it's all an illusion * Am feverishly curious...

So, if ya' ever meet me, and are at a loss for words, I invite you to strike up a chat on anything above. I'd enjoy it!

Love to all – Benjamin

An Invitation of Sorts

Congratulations, ya' made it to the end of my first attempt at authorship. I hope reading it was as pleasant as writing it.

Perhaps you would consider penning a short, impartial review (just a few words will do) offering others some insights on what to expect.

If amenable, I made it easy: Simply scan the QR Code or use the following link below. Once there, you'll find a *Review This Product* or *Write a Customer Review* option somewhere on the page.

https://www.amazon.com/dp/B08PDFXWHM

My Enduring Thanks!

Printed in Great Britain
by Amazon

26947731R00073